Diamond in the Dirt 2

By Carde'l

Book cover design by Justin Q Young
Book editing by Tiffany Horn

Published by Richard Jenkins for BLOCK STAR BOOKS

Printed in the United States of America

Carde'l contact info: *cardelunlimited@gmail.com*
Instagram: @CARD_E_L
Twitter: @CardelWrites
website: blockstar.blog

CHAPTER 1

KNOCK! KNOCK! KNOCK! "Who is it?!", Snake Eyes asked as he stood behind the door. "It's Real."

Snake Eyes unlocked the door.
"What's good li'l bro. Come in", Snake Eyes greeted smiling.
"I ain't mean to just pop up on you like this, but I ain't want to talk over them phones. I'm sure you already heard what happened", Real said.
"Yeah, them people came through and snatched my boy up. That's some straight bullshit."
"I know. He told me to come out here and pick up the rest of the money you owe him. I also got weight for sale if you need some."

A frown almost appeared on Snake Eyes face, but he caught himself. *What the fuck wrong with Benji leaving this little nigga out here with all the work?* Snake Eyes thought to himself highly upset and jealous.

Snake Eyes was certain Benji would've left the work and connect to him before anyone else being that he had been his most loyal and lucrative customer and business partner.

"You got work too huh? Well I need two keys."

"I only got one left, but anyway, where's that bread at Benji sent me out here to get?"

He must not have the connect, Snake Eyes thought. "Wait right here, I'm about to go grab it."

Snake Eyes darted into the kitchen and left through the back door. *I hope this nigga ain't on some other shit,* Real said to himself. He walked into the kitchen and grabbed a seat at the table. Within minutes, Snake Eyes came back through the door with a black duffle bag in his hand and sat it on the kitchen table in front of Real.

"That's 60 altogether. The $30 grand I owe Benji, and the $30 grand I'm spending on a key."

Real opened the duffle bag and counted the money. He stood up looking at Snake Eyes. "Aight, I'll be right back with that for you."

Real grabbed the duffle bag and rushed out of the house. He climbed back into the Porsche with Kaze, who was waiting impatiently. "Damn what took you so long? I was about to come up in there", Kaze said gripping the black .40 caliber handgun that rested on his lap.

Real smirked at how on point and trained to go his brother from another mother was. "Be easy bruh. He had to run to a different spot and grab the bread. Take me out the way to put this money up and grab this work for ole boy", Real said smoothly.

After Real dropped the money off at his sister's place, him and Kaze went back on the other side of the City to drop off the key for Snake Eyes.

"What's good li'l bro?" Roe said greeting Real after opening the door to the trap house. Roe was short, fat, and dark skin with a shiny bald head.

"Benji said he need all the bread you owe him", Real told him getting straight to the point.
"And who he sent over here to come get it, you?" Roe asked in disbelief with raised eyebrows.
"Yeah, me nigga! What the fuck!"

Them Fed charges drove Benji crazy already. He got this li'l ass nigga out here handling his money for him! Roe thought. He knew Benji would send someone to come pick the money up sooner or later, but the last person he expected it to be was Real's little young ass.

"I only got half right now."

Roe pulled a wad of cash out of his front pants pocket and handed it to Real, who quickly stuffed it in his pocket.
"Come through tomorrow and I should have the rest for you."

Real saw the big bulge in Roe's other front pocket, but he still nodded his head in agreement.

"Aight, you still got my cell number, right?"

"Yeah, I still got it. I'm gon' need some more coke too."

"I don't know how that's going to play out", Real told him before he stepped off the porch.

Real walked around the corner and hopped inside the Porsche.

"He gave you the money?" Kaze asked.

"He gave me half and told me to come get the other half from him tomorrow", Real said as he pulled the money out of his pocket to count it.

"That bitch ass nigga got the money right now. He think shit a game!"

Real felt his phone vibrating.

"Now who the hell is this."

Real placed the wad of cash on his lap. He looked at the screen and it was a text message from Dose in all caps. It read: I'M DONE WITH EVERYTHING.

"Shoot to the projects real quick. Dose said he done", Real said.

Kaze took Real to the trap spot to pick the money up from Dose. All they needed was the other 15 grand from Roe, and everything would be situated for Benji.

The next day it was drizzling outside. Real and Koze were both standing side by side in Tadasia's building hallway on the 3rd floor looking out of the window. "So when we gon' go get that bread from Roe's fat ass?" Kaze asked as he passed Real the pint of Hennessy.

"Probably a little...matter fact, I'm about to call him right now and let 'em know that we're on our way."

Real dialed Roe's number and then put the phone to his ear. It rung twice and then went to voicemail.

"I know this bitch ass nigga ain't just ignore my shit!"

Real twisted his face up as he pressed the TALK button again. This time without even ringing, it went straight to voicemail. Real hated when someone tried to play him.

"Man let's go around there", he stated angrily as he began walking down the stairwell.

"I told you that fat fuckhead was on some bullshit!" Kaze said as he followed him.

Real and Kaze both climbed inside the Porsche and sped out of the parking lot. Kaze parked around the corner from Roe's trap house. They were both already strapped down, wearing black Champion sweatshirts with the hoods pulled over their heads. As soon as Real and Kaze turned the corner, they saw a female fiend going inside Roe's trap house.

"Uh hum...his bitch ass in there, yo!" Kaze said. "Wait right here", Real ordered leaving Kaze standing on the corner.

Real strolled cautiously over to Roe's trap house. He looked around surveying his surroundings thoroughly before he slowly stepped onto the porch and knocked on the door. KNOCK! KNOCK! KNOCK! Real saw the blinds move, but no one came to the door. "This fat mufucka just don't know who he fucking with!" He mumbled angrily shaking his head as he stepped off the porch.

Kaze was already walking towards him. "Listen, I want you to go in the nigga back yard, and kick in the back door a few seconds after you hear the front window bust open", Real instructed in a low tone.

Kaze nodded his head in agreement, and then tied his hoodie tight around his face. He walked down the street and crept through the side of Roe's trap house, which led to the backyard. Real tightly tied the strings of his hoodie around his face picking up a brick from the side of the curb, and walked back to the front.

Meanwhile, Roe stood in the kitchen with his pants down while the skinny female fiend was on her knees giving him the best head job he had ever experienced in his life.

"Aww! Oh shit! Damn!" Roe groaned, closing his eyes and gripping the back of her head as she jerked his shaft and sucked on the head of his penis.

Suddenly the loud sound of glass shattering echoed throughout the house as a brick crashed though the living room window.
"What the fuck!" Roe exclaimed.

Roe began scrambling with his pants. His attention was on the loud sound that came from the living room. BOOM! Kaze shot the knob off and then crashed through the back door! Confused and extremely terrified, Roe continued to struggle with his pants as he made his way to the living room to grab the pistol he kept under the couch. BOOM! BOOM! BOOM!
"Agghh!" Roe yelled in agony.

Kaze pumped three slugs into Roe's back causing him to violently fall to the floor. His pants were halfway up so his black, ashy ass showed. The fiend was scared and in shock.

She tried to run and started screaming hysterically.

"You ain't think we was gon' come like this huh muhfucka?!" Kaze growled as he stood over top of Roe, who was sprawled on the floor bleeding profusely. Kaze turned to look at the fiend who was still screaming at the top of her lungs. He walked over and punched her in the mouth causing her to stumble back into the refrigerator.
"Shut ya crackhead ass up and go open the front door before I blow ya fucking head off!"

The fiend immediately shut up placing her hand over her bloody mouth and ran to open the door.

Real rushed in and quickly locked the door and immediately made his way to the kitchen. He had the shaken fiend by the neck at gunpoint. Kaze had already took everything that was inside of Roe's pockets.
"What the hell was going on in here?" Real asked looking down at Roe who was lying in a puddle of blood with his pants hanging

halfway off his ass! "This fat ass fuck boy was in here tricking with aunty", Kaze replied chuckling.

Real looked at the skinny fiend and shook his head in disgust.

"Please don't let me die! There's 200 grams in the cabinet over top of the sink, please call the ambulance!"

Real hurriedly grabbed the coke out of the cabinet before he and Kaze rushed out the back door.

Later on that night, Real met up with China Doll and gave her all the money Benji had left out on the streets. Real's exact words before getting out of China Doll's Aston Martin was, "Ask Benji how he gon' leave me the 'hood without leaving me with the plug to feed the 'hood!"

Roe survived the shooting but had to go through physical therapy to learn how to

walk again, and had to wear a shit bag the rest
of his life.

CHAPTER 2

Real and Kaze had grown tired of the Porsche, so they had Tadasia rent an all black Escalade truck with limo tints. After riding around all morning drinking Hennessy and listening to Jeezy's *Trap or Die* mix CD, Kaze decided to park across the street from the deli where they would usually stand to get their grind on. The tint was too dark to see inside the truck, and no one knew they had switched rentals, so no one knew they were posted on the block.

"Damn my nigga, pass the bottle!" Real demanded.

Kaze was guzzling the Henny like it was flavored water. He finally handed it to Real.
"Huh man, it ain't my fault you taking baby sips like you scared of the Henny."

Real chuckled as he took a gigantic gulp. A burning sensation rushed down his throat. His face twisted up as he grabbed his chest. Kaze burst out laughing. "Burn, don't it?!"

For the next 20 minutes, Real and Kaze bobbed their heads to Jeezy's lyrics while they surveyed everyone that came in and out of the deli. Real noticed a gray Buick slowly pull up and park on the side of the store. Two masked men climbed out of the backseat, wearing all black.

"Oh shit Kaze look!" Real tapped Kaze.

He turned down the volume and pointed towards the deli. Kaze saw the two masked men creeping on the side of the store with pistols in their hands.

"Who the fuck is that?" Kaze asked.

Kaze strained his eyes trying to see if anyone else was left inside the Buick. That's when he recognized Roe's little brother Zoe sitting in the driver's seat with his hands on the steering wheel.

"Oh shit! Them bitch ass niggas looking for us!" Kaze yelled.

He couldn't believe that Zoe and them little punk asses had the heart to come in their 'hood gunning for them. When Real looked at Zoe in the driver seat, he laughed.

"Man, they ain't even like that. Take me to go get my gun. It's my turn to bust some ass."

Kaze smiled as he pulled off looking at the gunmen come out of the store and get back into the Buick. Zoe and his goons tried to catch Real and Kaze slippin', but got caught slippin' in the process. Now Real and Kaze knew who was gunning for them, and the car they were riding in. If only Zoe and his goons knew they were parked across the street, it would've been the perfect opportunity, they were unarmed, off-point, and trapped in between two parked cars. It would've been impossible for Kaze to pull off in time.

An hour later, Real and Kaze sat in the Escalade six houses down from where Zoe, his baby's mother, and child lived. Real was in the back seat while Kaze sat in the driver's seat.

"Man, we should've just rode around until we spotted the car", Kaze said impatiently.

"Just chill, they going to pop up sooner or later, trust me", Real assured hoping that what Dynasty told him was true.

Dynasty and Zoe's baby mother, Toya, a jump-off to the highest degree, were close friends. Toya told Dynasty that Zoe must have heard about her sneaking dudes through the back door and letting them run trains on her while he was out hustling because he started popping up unexpectedly every few hours.

Finally, the grey Buick pulled up in front of the house. Real and Kaze watched as Zoe struggled to squeeze into his parking spot.
"There them niggas go right there!" Kaze said.

Kaze pulled off driving towards the Buick. Real felt his chest tighten and his palms began to sweat as he cocked back his Mac 10. CLICK CLACK!
"Roll the window down and stop at the side of the car", Real ordered.

Kaze did exactly what he was instructed to do. As soon as Real felt the truck stop, he quickly hung half of his body out of the window and began letting loose! TAT! TAT! TAT! TAT! TAT! TAT! TAT! TAT!

A gang of bullets ripped though the heads, necks, and chests of the young thugs sitting in the car, causing blood and brain fragments to splatter all over. The young thugs died instantly, but Zoe managed to get low, and only got hit in the shoulder.

Zoe opened the driver's side door and crawled out of the car in a panic. The burning sensation from the bullet traveled through his bloody shoulder. Zoe pulled his black 9mm off his hip as he got up from the ground and began busting back. BLOW! BLOW! BLOW! BLOW! BLOW! But it was too late, the Escalade was too far away!

Real and Dynasty sat side by side on the couch in front of the flat screen. Qadeesha and Kaze were in the back room with the door closed.
"Listen, me and Kaze was here with you and Qadeesha all day, and never left out the house

not even one time, you hear me?" Real said seriously looking Dynasty directly in her eyes.

"Alright, boy damn! I heard you the first, second, and third time. How many times you gon' say it?"

"I'm just trying to make sure you remember", Real said firmly.

"You act like you saying a whole lot. What I look slow? What you and Kaze did anyway?" She finally asked raising a suspicious eyebrow.

"We ain't do nothing", Real lied.

"Um hum…whateva!" Dynasty said rolling her eyes and sucking her teeth.

This boy want me to lie for him but he don't trust me enough to tell me what's going on, she said to herself as she noticed Real staring at her with a smirk on his face.

CHAPTER 3

Rays from the sun beamed down on Real's glistening 360 spinning waves making it look like his head was a bee's nest with honey on it. Kaze drove while Real sat in the passenger seat of the cherry red BMW convertible with the top down. He sipped on a bottle of Dom P, while bobbing his head to the 50 Cent and Akon's lyrics. *"Don't even look at me wrong when I come through the hood."*

"Damn she got a fat ass!" Real exclaimed. He removed his black Gucci shades from his wide eyes and watched the young lady's voluptuous booty jiggle in her white spandex pants as she sashayed down the street. Kaze caught a quick glimpse of the big booty.
"Damn", Kaze said in a whisper.

Kaze focused his eyes back on the road. He had his hair neatly braided in cornrows that hung near the middle of his back. Kaze turned down a side street and parked. He dug his hand in his all white linen pants pocket and pulled out a blunt and a bag of haze to roll up.

Even though he was parked in an unfamiliar area, someone creeping up trying to harm him and Real was the least of his worries. He had a black Glock 40 resting on the floor underneath his seat, and was begging for someone to give him a reason to use it. Ever since Real caught that double homicide, he was itching to catch one.

Kaze took a few puffs of his freshly rolled blunt and tried to pass it to Real.

"You know I don't smoke that shit", Real said.

Kaze chuckled as Real put the champagne bottle up to his mouth and took a gigantic gulp.

"I'm tired of riding around in this whack ass city. Let's go pick up Dynasty and Qadeesha, shoot to Philly, and have some fun", Real suggested.

Kaze felt his cell phone vibrating.

"This probably them right here...Yo?" Kaze answered.

"Hey babes, what's going on with you?" Kia asked in a sweet tone.

Kaze heard her voice and tapped Real, who was staring at a group of people that were having a cookout in their front yard a few houses down.

"Not too much...me and my brother from another mother just riding around with the top down enjoying this beautiful weather, nah mean."

"Oh shit, girl they riding around in a drop top", Kia whispered to her best friend Tia without Kaze being able to hear.

"What's up for today? Y'all act like y'all scared of me and my girl or something!" Kia said.

"Scared huh. Kamikaze don't know how to be scared."

Kaze put the blunt of haze to his lips, took a pull, and blew the smoke into the air.

"Well me and Tia together, y'all can come and get us right now if it's all like that."

"Where y'all at?"

"We at 157 Greenwood. Come through…"

"Aight, we on our way right now..." Kaze assured before hanging up and looking at Real.

Real was staring right back.
"Why would you tell them we on our way when we about to pick up Dynasty and Qadeesha?" Real asked.

Kaze waited for a few seconds trying to think of what to say.
"Because we just took them to Philly last week!"
"So what? We don't even know them groupie hoes" Real argued.

After going back and forth with Kaze for 10 minutes, Real finally gave in and agreed to take Tia and Kia to Philly.

When they arrived in Philly, they rode around for a few hours smoking weed and getting drunk, before finally going to a Chinese restaurant. Oriental music streamed throughout the busy restaurant as the waitresses went from table to table taking everyone's order and dropping food off. Real and Kaze sat side by side directly across from their dates at the first table inside near a window.

"Damn this shit good as hell!" Kaze stated.

Kaze dug his spoon into his plate. His eyes were blood shot from the three dutches of haze he smoked to the head while everyone else was just feeling nice off the back to back bottles of Dom P they drank. "Yeah the food is banging here", Real agreed as he picked up the lemon pepper chicken wing from his glass plate and took a big bite.

He looked at the ladies and smirked at how they were munching down on their food without saying one word. It definitely was no shame in their game.
"I see y'all two feel the same way", Real said before taking a sip of his iced tea lemonade.

Both Tia and Kia nodded in agreement while still munching. Unbeknownst to them, they caught a contact from the haze Kaze smoked in the car.

It did not take long for everyone to finish their food.
"Damn, today seems like it went by fast as hell", Kaze said while stretching his arms out.
"Yeah, I know right", Kia agreed licking her lips, staring into Kaze's red eyes.

Kia then slid her tiny foot out of her flip flop and rubbed it between Kaze's legs causing him to jump. "Whoa", he uttered in a whisper.

Kaze's manhood rose instantly as he noticed the naughty grin on Kia's face. She had been teasing Kaze all day, which had him under the impression that it would be on between the two of them later on. Kaze looked at Real and Tia who were deep into their own conversation.
"Let's get out of here", he said.

Once Kaze paid the bill he stood up from his seat, grabbed hold of Kia's hand, and strolled out of the restaurant. Tia and Real followed behind them. The sun was setting as the two couples strolled through the parking lot holding hands. *I'm gon' bust her ass tonight*, Kaze said to himself looking over his shoulder at Real.

"What hotel you want to go to bruh?" Kaze asked.
"I'm not going to no hotel with you on the first date boy! What I look like?!" Kia frowned.

Kaze stopped in mid step and looked at Kia like she had lost her damn mind.
"What you mean you ain't going to no hotel?"
"Exactly what I just said!"

Real, who was still holding Tia's hand, sighed out loud and shook his head as he stopped in his tracks to watch Kaze and Kia continuously go back and forth. All you heard was their loud voices screaming at each other throughout the parking lot.

Seeing that things were getting out of hand, Real released his hand from Tia's grasp, and stepped between Kaze and Kia.

"Kaze chill out bruh. You tripping right now!" Real said raising his voice as he stood face to face with his brother.

"I ain't tripping. That bitch tripping! It's either we going to get a room or I'm leaving her ass right here in this parking lot."

Even though Kia was flirting with him, the mixture of the liquor and weed had him taking things overboard. Kia started crying as Tia stepped close beside her.

"Why is he acting like that?" Tia asked.

"That bitch know why I'm acting like this! She been teasing me all night, acting like she wanted to give me the pussy. Now she on some funny shit. Man fuck her!" Kaze hollered harshly before he got in the car.

Kaze grabbed the pint of Henny out of the passenger's seat and kept taking swigs until it was almost empty.

"Hold on real quick", Real said to the ladies looking at Tia who was comforting Kia while she cried like a baby.

Real walked over to the car and opened the driver side door.
"You on some real live bullshit right now, you know that? For one, you too drunk to drive."

Real snatched the bottle out of Kaze's hand while he was still attempting to drink out of it, causing a little to spill on his expensive pants.

"For two, niggas like us don't stress no broad over no pussy. What you lost ya mind nigga? Now calm down and come on."

Real wrapped Kaze's arm around his shoulder and helped him get into the backseat before turning to Tia.
"Do you know how to drive?"
"Yeah", Tia answered.
"You and Kia get in the front, I'm gon' get in the back with Kaze."

Tia and Kia did exactly what they were told and pulled out of the parking lot. Everyone sat in complete silence for the entire ride back to Trenton.

Real's eyes slowly cracked open once he felt the car come to a stop.
"We finally here, huh?" he said as he looked out of the window and noticed that they were in front of Tia's house.
Real stretched and yawned before he turned to look at Kaze, who was snoring lightly with his head resting on the car door.

"Yup, finally here", Tia responded before she and Kia got out of the car.

Real got to walk them to the porch.
"Y'all have to excuse my brother Kamikaze. He really didn't mean any harm, he was just drunk and horny I guess", Real said trying to lighten things up as he walked in between the two girls.

"Don't worry we'll be aight. We have been through way worse, trust me!" Tia admitted.

Kia walked ahead up the porch steps, while Tia stopped and turned around to face Real.
"I enjoyed spending the day with you and I'm really looking forward to a next time", Tia told him before sticking her tongue down his throat.

Caught completely off guard, Real just followed the rhythm of her tongue and wrapped his hands around her lower waist.

"Oh! So this who you been with, huh bitch?!"

The voice startled Tia, and she immediately got nervous when she recognized her boyfriend's deep voice.
"Oh shit! Ricky!"

Ricky had crept up on Real and Tia from the side of the house, along with two other young thugs from his neighborhood.

"Here this nigga go with this nut shit again", Real murmured to himself, not knowing what to expect.

As Tia walked towards Ricky, he stormed her way. "Baby, I'm sorry. We were just riding around!"

The palm of Ricky's hand forcefully came across her face.
"Aghh", she screamed as she fell to the ground, holding the side of her face.

"Oh my gosh Tia!" Kia hollered as she rushed off the porch to help her friend get up from off the ground.

Just as Real was about to step in and help, Ricky charged him and swung a wild right hook. Real side stepped it, and hit him with a mean on-banger, causing Ricky to fall down to the ground. Real quickly turned to the two young thugs that were hesitantly approaching him. He planted his feet and put his guard up. "What y'all waiting for? Come on!" Real taunted.

Suddenly, Real felt an extremely sharp pain in his lower back.

"Agghh!" he groaned dropping down to one knee and reaching for his lower back where the excruciating pain was. BOOM!

Real turned to see Ricky's brains splatter out of his head as he slowly fell to the ground face first, holding a bloody knife in his hand. He then looked up and saw Kaze standing over top of Ricky's body with the smoking Glock 40 in his hand. Kaze looked to his left and noticed the two young thugs that came along with Ricky making a run for it. BLOW! BLOW! BLOW! He aimed his gun in their direction and let off several shots just barely missing them.

"Fuck!" Kaze yelled in frustration, realizing they may go to the police.

Kaze carefully scanned the area and noticed Tia and Kia's eyes staring directly at him. He walked up on the two frightened girls who were shaking uncontrollably, and pointed the gun at Tia's head.

"No!" Kia screamed knowing she would be next.

Real was still down on one knee watching from a few feet away. He wanted to tell Kaze to fall back but the intense pain in his lower back made him unable to speak.

Kaze pulled the trigger. CLICK! He was so deep into his murderous zone, that he didn't even realize he had emptied the clip and the gun reclined. Kaze was completely pissed off.
"You bitches ain't see nothing right?" He asked with clenched teeth.
"No Kaze, we ain't see nothing! We ain't see nothing! Please!"

Tia and Kia could not stop crying, they were scared for their lives. Their response is all Kaze wanted to hear before he rushed to Real's aid. He put Real in the car and fled the scene, speeding off recklessly to the hospital.

Kaze dropped Real off at the emergency room. He then drove to pick up Qadeesha to hide out just in case someone started snitching.

Real was lying down in the hospital bed when he slowly opened his eyes. He made an attempt to move his arm, but couldn't because it was hand cuffed to the bed.

"You had a rough night huh?" An unfamiliar voice said.

Startled, Real looked to his left and saw two detectives seated in the hospital chairs next to his bedside. One of the detectives was a short and chubby Puerto Rican man with a neat low cut.

"I hate to be the bearer of bad news, but you're being charged with conspiracy to murder!" The black detective informed, staring at Real trying to read his facial expression.

After hearing what the detective said, Real was hoping he was dreaming and someone was about to wake him up. It couldn't get any worse than it already was. He was stabbed in the back over a female that he barely knew, and now was being charged with a murder that he didn't even commit. *What the fuck! I ain't never coming home!,* Real thought as a somber feeling came over him. Real stared back at the detective with a straight face.

"Real, you have a chance to help yourself. We know you're not the shooter", the black detective said.

"Fuck y'all. I ain't telling y'all shit! Matter fact, y'all not even supposed to be talking to me. I'm a juvenile! Once my lawyer..."

Before Real could finish his sentence, the black detective interrupted him.

"Your guardian gave us permission to talk to you."

Real sighed out loud as he looked away. *What the hell she do that for,* Real thought.

"So where is she?" Real asked.

"She's out in the hallway", the Puerto Rican detective replied.

"Aight, I'm done talking to y'all. Tell her to come in on y'all way out!" Real shut down.

"Alright son, it's your choice, but if you ever have a change of heart, you know our number."

Before the detectives could fully exit the room, Tadasia and Dynasty walked in and had a seat next to Real's bedside.

"Why you give them fuck heads permission to talk to me? I ain't got nothing to talk to them about."

Tadasia wasn't even aware she gave the detectives permission, all she knew is that she was worried and scared for her brother. She really didn't know what to do or say.

"What happened?" Tadasia asked ignoring all that Real just said.

"I don't know", he lied.

He couldn't tell his sister what happened, especially with Dynasty present in the room.

"All I remember is feeling a sharp pain in my back, and then falling to the ground."

Real looked at Dynasty, who was staring at him with sad eyes, and immediately a feeling of guilt came over him. Not only would

Dynasty's heart be broken in to pieces if Real told them what really happened, but she probably would've walked out of his life during a time he needed her the most.

"Where's Kaze", he asked.
"I don't know where his crazy ass at. He called me last night and told me you got stabbed and was being held here."

Meanwhile, the sound of car horns echoed through the air from traffic as crowds of people walked up and down the street. Kaze and Qadeesha stood dead smack in the center of downtown Philly in front of a pizza shop.
"Call Dynasty and see what's up with Real", Kaze ordered before he took a bite of pizza.

Qadeesha, who stood close beside him, pulled out her cell and called her friend.
"Hello."

Kaze stared at Qadeesha while she spoke on the phone. He could tell by her sad facial expression that something bad happened.
"What happened?" He asked anxiously.

Qadeesha lifted her index finger signaling for him to wait a minute. Kaze shook his head from side to side. Qadeesha finally hung up.

"Dynasty said that Real's ok, but the detectives charged him with conspiracy to murder, and that they are looking for you."

Qadeesha 's voice was cracking as the tears began rolling down her soft brown cheeks. She had a feeling there was more to the story than what Kaze told her, and the information she just received confirmed it.
"They're saying that you're the shooter."
"Fuck!" Kaze yelled.

Kaze slammed his pizza on the ground and ran his hand over top of his head. Some of the people walking down the congested street looked at Kaze like he was crazy. *I knew them bitches was gon' run they mouths! It's aight though. 'I got something for they asses!* Koze thought to himself.

"Kaze what you went and did now?" Qadeesha asked between sniffles.

"I ain't do nothing. Now listen to what I'm about to say to you. I'm about to drop you off in the city. I want you to go home and get some money out of my stash, then call my mom and tell her I said to get me a lawyer."

"I'm not leaving you. I'm going everywhere you're going."

"You can't go where I'm about to go. Just do what I told you to do!" Kaze ordered raising his voice in frustration.

A few hours had passed, and it was finally getting dark outside. Kaze was wearing a black Champion sweatshirt with the hood tied tightly around his face. He crept quietly on the side of Tia's house, heading towards the backyard. He held a black .357 Magnum in his hand. Kaze stopped in his tracks when he noticed a window propped open, and decided to take a peek. *Just in time*, he thought when he saw Tia and Kia sitting in the living room watching TV.

"Girl, I'm about to go get something to drink", Kia said to Tia who was still mourning over the tragic incident that occurred.

Kia stood up and walked into the kitchen. Kaze quickly dipped to the side so she wouldn't see him, and rushed to the backyard. He was about to shoot the door knob off and rush inside, but something told him to check the door first. Kaze grabbed the door knob and was surprised to see that it was unlocked. *This gon' be easier than I thought,* Kaze said to himself with a devilish grin on his face. He quietly turned the knob, and snuck in to the house. Kia had her back to the door and was reaching for a carton of orange juice from out the refrigerator.

Kaze slowly walked up behind Kia and forcefully put his hand over her mouth, pointing the .357 at her head. Kia's eyes grew wide as she jumped and dropped the carton of orange juice on the floor. Her heart was beating rapidly.

"Scream and I'll blow ya fucking head off", Kaze whispered in her ear in a menacing tone.

Hot tears slid down Kia's cheeks and onto Kaze's hand.

"How many people in this fucking house?"

Kia lifted her trembling hand and raised one finger... Tia.

"What's going on in there girl? What, you dropped something?...Kia?" Tia shouted from the living room.

Kaze heard footsteps and knew that Tia was on her way in to the kitchen. With his hand still covering Kia's mouth, Kaze leaned up against the side of the wall near the kitchen entrance and made Kia lie on the floor. As soon as Tia entered the kitchen, Kaze violently grabbed her by the hair. She screamed trying to break free from his grasp.

"Shut the fuck up!" Kaze growled as he forcefully swung her by her hair down to the floor.

"Aaghh", Tia screamed.

Tia looked up and recognized that it was Kaze by his lips and nose. This made her more afraid then she already was. She knew this time he wasn't going to run out of bullets.

Tia and Kia were shaking and crying hysterically as they held on to each other. They looked up into Kaze's crazed blood shot eyes.
"I let y'all bitches live, and y'all snitch on me and my brother!"
Kaze aimed the gun at Tia's head.

"We...we...we didn't tell the police anything when they came here! We...we said we didn't know who y'all was or seen y'all faces!" Tia stuttered.

Tia was so afraid she could barely get her words together.

"You lying bitch!!" Kaze yelled harshly as spit flew out of his mouth.

Tia put her hands up blocking her face as if she could block a bullet.

"Please Kaze! Don't kill us! I swear on my dead mother's grave we didn't tell. It had to be Li'l L and Double R! They be on Hampton hustling all day and all night!"

Kaze stared intensely at the two young ladies for a few seconds, trying to get a read on them to see if they were feeding him some bullshit or not. *Maybe it was them bitch ass niggas,* he thought to himself.

Kaze looked around and noticed some pictures on the refrigerator. It was a picture of Tia's little brother and sister. He snatched them from off the refrigerator and stuffed them into his pocket.
"If y'all lying I'll be back and I ain't doing no talking! I'm killing the whole house!!" Kaze threatened before he ran out the back door.

Kaze parked around the corner from Hampton Ave. He got out of the vehicle and started speed walking with his hands tucked inside his front hoodie pocket. Kaze walked down Hampton when he noticed three young thugs standing on the porch of the house that

Tia said Lil L and Double R were hustling out of. Kaze never did get a good look at their faces, so he didn't know if it was them or not.

"A yo? You niggas seen Li'l L and Double R out here?" Kaze asked looking up at the three young thugs standing a few feet away from the porch steps.

They were all sipping on personal bottles of Remy Martin and had very depressed looks on their faces, as if they were mourning over Ricky.

"Nah, they ain't been out here all day", one of the young thugs said sadly without even looking at Kaze.

"Well, I need you to give them a message for me!"

Kaze pulled his gun out and started letting loose recklessly. BLOW! BLOW! BLOW! BLOW! All three ducked for cover as slugs knocked chunks of wood out of the wooden door!

Kaze emptied all his bullets and began running to his car. Suddenly, he spotted a blue unmarked car swinging around the corner. Hearing the loud gunshots and seeing Kaze running, the undercover detectives immediately turned on the sirens and gave chase.
"Oh shit!" He yelled.

Kaze glanced back at the car speeding towards him. He knew he wasn't going be able to make it to his car without getting caught so he cut through the side of a brick house and jumped the fence in the backyard, which put him in the middle of an alley.

Breathing heavily, Kaze threw the heavy .357 as hard as he could. It landed on top of an abandoned building. He started running again when a burgundy unmarked car and and a black unmarked car came speeding from both ends of the alley, trapping Kaze in. *Damn man! I hope they ain't see me throw the gun!* Kaze thought panicking.

Both of the cars were still coming at him full speed. In fear of getting ran over, Kaze backed up into another backyard. He dropped down to his knee and placed both of his hands on his head in surrender. The cars came to a screeching halt, and detectives hopped out of each car with their guns drawn.

"On the ground!" One of the detectives yelled as they cautiously stepped towards Kaze in hopes he'd make a false move so he could send a bullet through the back of his head.

CHAPTER 4

Real and Kaze were being held at the Juvenile Correctional Center and were now in the chow hall eating the garbage they served for lunch. They sat across from each other at the table near the large red juice container.

"Damn man, I told you we should've just stuck to what we were doing instead of fucking with them silly ass hoes! Now look where we at, and look at the bullshit we wearing!" Real complained.

Real and Kaze were dressed in black bobo sneakers with the dark green pants and short sleeve shirt that the facility provided to all the inmates. Real scooped up a spoon full of mashed potatoes from his tray and put them into his mouth. The stab wound was still fresh, so it hurt like hell when he moved in certain positions. Kaze hung his head low as he played with the food in his tray.

"Yeah man, I know", Kaze said sadly.

Kaze felt like if it wasn't for him, things wouldn't have turned out the way that they had. When Kaze was apprehended, the detective's didn't find the gun that he threw, nor had any witnesses come forward. They had no real evidence to connect him with the murder or the shooting.

"I can't eat no more of this bullshit. It feels like I'm about to throw up", Real said dropping the spoon on to his tray.

Real grabbed his white plastic cup and took a sip of the blue juice.

"When is the lawyer coming up here to see us?" Kaze asked.
"Supposed to be today", Real replied.

Kaze waited for a few seconds before he spoke again. "Man it don't make no sense for both of us to go down for this shit. I'm telling my lawyer that I want to take the weight for everything in order to let you go. The shit mostly my fault anyway. Hopefully, I get something light. If not, fuck it. I'm still young, I'll be home. All I ask for you to do is hold down me, my mom, and Qadeesha while I'm doing my time."

Kaze was dead serious. He had made the decision a few days ago, and decided now would be the perfect time to bring it up. Real shook his head in disagreement.
"Nah bruh, we in this shit together."
"...And we still gon' be in this shit together. You gon' hold it up out there for the both of us, and I'm gon' hold it down in here, nah mean? I..."

Just then, a short light skin female staff member approached their table.
"Mr. Johnson and Mr. Vega y'all have an attorney visit."

The two friends looked at each other.
"Come on", Kaze ordered eagerly.

Real and Kaze quickly got up and followed their escort out of the chow hall and down the long corridor. They finally stopped in front of two doors leading to two different rooms. The escort turned to face them.

"Mr. Johnson you're in this room, and Mr. Vega you're in here."

Kaze and Real entered their assigned rooms. Kaze took a seat across from his attorney. He was a white man with jet black hair, wearing a black suit and a red tie.

"How are you doing Mr. Vega? I'm Mr. Lustbader, I'll be representing you on your case", Mr. Lustbader introduced while holding his hand out.

"I'm good", Kaze replied shaking his hand.

Mr. Lustbader was a very money hungry Jewish lawyer. He was known throughout New Jersey as the *'Jewish Bull'* in the court room. Kaze's mother, Carla, used the money Qadeesha gave her plus cash from her own pocket to get her son one of the best lawyers money could buy. She wasn't just going to let the administration smoke her son like dirt weed.

Before Mr. Lustbader could get a chance to explain the details of the case, Kaze had something he wanted to say.

"Listen, I ain't trying to make your job harder than it already is. I got an extra 10 grand for you if you can beat my waiver and get me anywhere from a 4 to 7 year sentence. I'll take the weight for everything and let my co-d walk. He ain't have nothing to do with it."

The lawyer remained silent for a few seconds before he responded.
"Well, um, I'm not going to make any promises, but there's a strong possibility things will work out in your favor."

The possibility of Kaze getting what he wanted was stronger than Mr. Lustbader made it seem. He had plans on squeezing a few extra grand out of the young gangster's pockets.

"Aight, check into whatever you got to check into, then come back and holla at me", Kaze told him smiling.

Even though the deal wasn't 100% guaranteed, just knowing that things could work out in his favor made Kaze feel a whole lot better than he was feeling before he walked through that door.

"I need to talk to your co-defendant's lawyer and the prosecutor. When that's done we should be able to put things in motion. I'll send you a letter once everything goes through", Lustbader said rising.

Kaze nodded his head as he stood to shake the lawyer's hand. When he opened the door and stepped out of the conference room, he saw Real standing next to their escort.

"What did ya lawyer say?" Real asked.
"He said that he had to talk to your lawyer and the prosecutor before he could tell me whether or not he could make it happen."
"Make what happen?"

Real didn't think that Kaze discussed the deal to take the charge so soon. Kaze noticed that the escort was ear hustling.
"I'm gon' tell you everything when we get on the tier."

When they finally reached their cell Kaze explained everything he discussed with his lawyer, and Real told him everything as well.

9 days had gone by and everything was going as well as could be expected. Real and Kaze were in the chow hall sitting laughing and cracking jokes while eating their food. Out of no where, a short brown skinned cocky young thug approached their table.
"Ay yo, which one of y'all name is Kaze?"

Kaze turned to look at the young thug.
"Why? Who wants..."

Before Kaze could finish his sentence, a hard right hook came crashing across his jaw, causing him to slide out of his chair and fall to the floor! Real managed to slide out of his seat and swing a bo-low that connected to the young thug's rib cage.
"Aggh!"

The young thug groaned in agony as he grabbed his side and fell to the ground. By that time, most of the kids eating jumped out of their seats to watch the fight. A gang of kids from the young thug's area rushed towards the scuffle to help their homeboy.

Real stepped to the young thug getting ready to kick him in the face, but a wild punch came from behind that landed directly on his chin causing Real to stumble backwards. Suddenly he felt an extremely sharp pain in his lower back near his stab wound. "Aggh!"

Real held his wound as he dropped down to one knee. He felt a shoe crash against his ribs causing him to grasp his side and curl up on the ground. The group of young thugs stood over him and began stomping him. Real was balled up trying to protect his face the best he could, but he saw Kaze curled up on the ground a few feet away getting stomped too.

Finally, a group of staff members rushed over to break up the fight, taking everyone to lock up. They had put Real and Kaze in the same cell together.

"You aight my nigga?" Kaze asked.

"Yeah, I'm good. My back just feels fucked up!"

Real limped to the mirror with his hand on his back and became extremely furious when he saw his swollen black eye.

"I'm gon' murder one of them niggas as soon as I come home! Look at my eye!" Real yelled angrily raising his voice meaning every word he said.

Kaze looked to see, all he had was a swollen lip.

"Damn! That shit look crazy bruh."

All of a sudden, they heard someone screaming Kaze's name.

"Kaze! Kaze! I know you hear me you bitch ass nigga!"

The unfamiliar voice caused Kaze to rush to his cell door. He looked through the plexiglass and saw the young thug that knocked him out standing in front of the cell door directly across from him. This made Kaze's blood boil, he wasn't used to dudes having one up on him. The young thug continued to shout through the door.

"There ya bitch ass go! The nigga you locked up for killing was from my 'hood nigga! You know what it is!"

Kaze put his mouth to the crack of the door and shouted back.

"I ain't with that lip gangster screaming behind the door shit. We gon' do us when these doors bust open!"

A few hours later, Real and Kaze were both lying in their bunks talking about how much they missed their girlfriends and the comforts of home. A staff member tapped on their cell door.

"Mail up!"

The staff member slid 4 envelopes under the door. Real, who was lying on the bottom bunk, slowly got up to gather the letters from off the floor. A wide smile came across his face after he read the names written on the envelopes. They both had letters from their girls and their attorneys. Kaze anxiously sat up when he saw the wide grin on Real's face and said, "Who is it from?"

Without saying a word, Real handed Kaze his two letters before sitting on his bunk to read his. Kaze also began reading his letter from Lustbader.

Mr. Vega,

Your request was brought to the prosecutor's attention. Your willingness to satisfy the indictment under the conditions you requested is granted without argument. He has agreed to your terms. You are scheduled to appear before the judge, September 17, 2006.

Regards,
Mr. Alan Lustbader

"Oh shit. They gon' let me take the charge!" Kaze exclaimed excitedly before hopping off the top bunk. "Word up? Let me see what my lawyer talking about."

Real placed Dynasty's letter on his lap and grabbed the letter from his attorney. He skimmed through it real quick.

"Yeah, you right, but our court date far as hell."

The court date was finally here. Kaze's and Real's shackled legs shuffled through the court room door. Wide smiles appeared on their faces when they saw Carla, Qadeesha, Candace, Tadasia, and Dynasty sitting on the bench in the front row. The two young gangsters waved their shackled hands at their families as they followed the officer that escorted them.

Their attorneys stood behind the defense table conversing.

"That must be the prosecutor. Now tell me he don't look like Pee Wee Herman?" Kaze said jokingly.

Real took one look and almost burst into laughter., but he caught himself. The man looked exactly like Pee Wee Herman. He wore the same exact gray suit and everything, all he was missing was the red bow tie. He wore a blue one instead.

Mr. Lustbader walked over with a green sheet of paper in his hand and took a seat on the wooden bench right next to Kaze. He explained the procedures for taking a plea before having him sign his cop-out papers.
"Your co-defendant's lawyer will let him know he doesn't have to do anything but sit there."

Everyone present inside the courtroom immediately got quiet when they saw the judge enter through the side door and take his seat. He was a chubby older white man with a bald head.

"All Rise!" The bailiff announced.

The judge took his seat.
"Everyone may be seated."

The judge put on his glasses and began searching through sheets of paper before him. Kaze and Real's case was heard first.

"Alright...Mr. Stevens and Mr. Lustbader come forward. From my understanding Mr. Vega is pleading to the charges and is willing to take a plea offer, correct?"

"Yes your honor, Mr. Vega is here to plead guilty to aggravated manslaughter with a sentence of juvenile life in which he will serve a mandatory four years before he is eligible for parole. We are requesting that all charges be dismissed against Mr. Johnson since he was unconscious from a life-threatening stab wound when the crime was committed", the prosecutor explained.

The judge nodded his head. "Very well. Mr. Lustbader any objections?"

"No, your honor."

"How about you Mr. Lorde, any objections?" The judge asked Real's lawyer.

"No, I'm good your honor."

The judge cleared his throat.

"Mr. Vega, please stand."

Kaze's matted french braid caused him to have a scruffy appearance. He stood up with his head held high and looked the judge directly in to his blue eyes. However, when the judge began to speak Kaze suddenly felt a nervous energy in the pit of his stomach.

"Sir, in your own words are you pleading to this charge? The Aggravated Manslaughter of Ricky Burnett, the victim?"
Kaze took a deep breath and looked at his mother and his girl before turning back to the judge. Admitting to murdering someone in front of his mother and everyone else in the courtroom made him feel awkward and ashamed but he knew he had to do what he had to do.

"Yes sir. I am. Can I say a few words, sir?" Kaze requested.

The judge reminded him that he is still under oath, and that he could be charged with further incidence.

"I just want to set the record straight that Real Johnson was unconscious during the incident sir. He had been stabbed by Ricky Burnett and was on the ground in a pool of blood. So that's when I got out my car and shot him in the head. I was only trying to keep him from killing my friend. After that, I picked Real up and put him inside the car and dropped him off at the hospital", Kaze explained.

"Do you know why Mr. Burnett would have wanted to stab Mr. Johnson?" the judge asked.

Fuck! Man if I tell'em why Ricky stabbed Real Dynasty and Qadeesha gon' be on some real live bullshit. I hope he dont already know, Kaze thought to himself in a panic as he glanced at Qadeesha and then at Real. Kaze could tell that Real was thinking the same exact thing. "No your honor'", Kaze replied.
"Alright, you may be seated.

The judge knew that the two young gangsters were lying but he didn't care. His main concern was to move on to the next case and get the day over with. He sent them on their way in minutes, and before long the sound of Kaze and Real's shackles rattled as they followed their escort out of the courtroom.

Real was released immediately to Tadasia's custody upon reaching the Juvenile facility.
"Your ride is outside waiting for you", the staff member yelled from his desk.

Real was happy that he was going home but he also felt bad about leaving his partner in crime behind. Things definitely weren't going to be the same without Kaze, the loose cannon, around. Real stood just a few feet away from Kaze, holding his packed bag. Kaze felt satisfied about taking the charge. He was what you called a real stand up gangster.

"Damn bruh, what you 'bout to bust out and cry on me?" Kaze asked when he noticed the sad look on Real's face.
"Nah, it just feel fucked up leaving you in here like this."
"Man this ain't about nothing. I'll be back out on them streets my first eligibility date. You just got to get out there, get that connect from

Benji, and turn it the fuck up! All I ask for you to do is look out for my mom and my girl", Kaze reminded him. "Oh yeah, you can flip that bread Qadeesha got at the crib if you want to."

Kaze and Real slapped hands and embraced. The staff member popped up in the door way. "Boy, you better hurry up and come on before they do count!"

Real grabbed his pillow and sheets. "Alright bruh, you'll be hearing from me soon", Real said. "Don't forget to holla at them niggas that tried to get a one up on us in here", Kaze shouted as Real rushed out the cell and off the tier.

When Real stepped through the jail gate, he saw his sister and Dynasty sitting on the hood of his Cadillac smiling. "Hey little brother, it feels good to be out don't it?" Tadasia asked joyfully as she stood up and gave Real a hug.

Words couldn't describe how happy Tadasia was about her little brother making it out of this unfortunate situation. She didn't want him doing anything that could land him back in jail.

"Now you just got to stay out here and away from the bullshit."

"Oh that's one thing you ain't gotta worry about Tadasia. He ain't going no where without me", Dynasty assured before she gave Real a hug and kiss on the lips.

Real was locked in Dynasty's embrace when he looked into her eyes. Dynasty stared back.

"Yup, everywhere."

Tadasia started laughing at Dynasty's dominant attitude.

"That's right! Lock his ass down, girl!"

Tadasia opened the driver side door and slid inside the car. Real hopped in the back and Dynasty sat in the passenger seat before Tadasia pulled out of the parking lot.

Once Tadasia dropped herself off in front of her building, Real realized that he actually did need Dynasty to be everywhere he went. He still hadn't learned how to drive and didn't trust anyone else enough to roll with him when he made moves.

Dynasty drove Real to Qadeesha's house to pick up Kaze's money, then to the nearest Chinese store to grab a bite to eat before finally going to Dynasty's house. As soon as they stepped inside the apartment they took a shower together and ate their Chinese food in the kitchen at the dinner table. Once they finished, Real gently grabbed Dynasty by the hand and led her to the living room, where they both sat on the leather couch and had a very serious talk. Real filled her in on all his plans and explained to her everything he knew about the game. She was going to be running the streets with him as his ride or die, so he had to make sure that she understood exactly what it involved.

Later that night, Real and Dynasty suited up in all black and went for a ride on the other side of the city. Dynasty parked around the corner from the block Real's enemies hustled on. Real sat in the passenger seat holding two chrome .40 caliber handguns. They both had on black masks.

"Aight babes, now listen. When you get near the red brick house, I want you to drive real slow until I tell you to pull off", Real explained carefully.

Dynasty had butterflies in her stomach but still nodded her head.
"Alright, I know what to do."

As Dynasty pulled off, her chest tightened up and her heart started beating rapidly when she saw the big crowd of hustlers standing in front of the brick house. She did exactly what she was instructed to do.

"Bitch ass niggas!" Real shouted while standing up through the sunroof.
Real aimed at the crowd and began letting go.
BLOW! BLOW! BLOW! BLOW! BLOW! BLOW! BLOW! BLOW! BLOW!

The shiny chrome from the twin .40 cals glistened in the darkness as sparks of fire continuously blew out of the barrels. A gang of slugs ripped through two of the young thug's chest that stood in front of the brick house, causing them to stumble back and violently fall against the wall. Everyone in the crowd stampeded, ducking and dodging and running as fast as they could, hoping that they weren't going to be the next to get hit. Real had definitely caught them by surprise.

"Pull off!" Real ordered, satisfied after emptying both clips.

Real slid his upper body back into the car. Dynasty slammed her foot on the gas pedal causing the tires to screech as she sped off and turned the corner recklessly.

First day home and Real kept his word and did exactly what he said he was going to do. Although he didn't get at the same exact dudes that smashed him and Kaze out in the chow hall, he still laid somebody down from their hood, which was good enough for the time being.

After putting in serious work, Real and Dynasty went straight to Real's sister apartment. There Real called China Doll and told her to tell Benji that he was home, and needed some work.

Two weeks later, Dynasty cruised through the shady streets of Trenton, while Real was leaned back in his seat sipping a pint of Hennessy bobbing his head as Lloyd Banks lyrics blared through the speakers.
"If you my nigga, you my nigga to the end."

The music made him reminisce about all the good times and the hard times he and his brother from another mother had shared together.

Damn, my nigga ain't gon' be out here on these streets with me for a minute, Real thought to himself sadly as he took another sip of the Henny. Everything just felt awkward without Kaze being around.

Dynasty took her eyes off the road to glance at Real and could tell by the look on his face that something was bothering him. "Baby, you aight?" she asked as she focused back on the road.

"Yeah, I'm good." Real felt his phone vibrating. "Yo?"

"Hey Real", China Doll greeted, "I got a letter for you from your big brother."

"Word up?" Real said excitedly with raised eyebrows as he glanced at Dynasty.

China Doll laughed at Real's excitement. "Yeah, where do you want to meet up at so I can give it to you?" She asked.

"Meet me at the spot you dropped me off at before I got locked up", Real suggested.

"Aight, I'm on my way now."

"Ride up to the projects real quick babes, so I can get this letter from Benji's girl", Real demanded eagerly.

Real couldn't wait to see what Benji was talking about. Dynasty made a U-turn in the middle of the street and headed to the projects parking lot. They waited 20 minutes for China Doll, who finally pulled up and parked nearby. Real hopped out of his car and into hers.

"What's good?" Real greeted as he closed the passenger door.

"Same shit. Here the letter he wrote you."

China Doll handed real Benji's letter. Real ripped the envelope, took the letter out and read it.

China Doll will give you the number to the plug. He's already waiting for you to call. Remember, Real niggaz make shit happen.

Benji the Breadwinner!

While Real was reading, China Doll was in the mirror applying lipgloss to her full pink lips.

"I talked to him today, he said stay out of the bullshit and just get money. Here go the number."

Real nodded his head in agreement and took the small piece of paper and tucked it in his pocket.

"Aight China Doll, call me if you need anything", Real said as he exited the pink Aston Martin.

He was so in a rush to call the plug he forgot to send his thanks to Benji. Real noticed the look on Dynasty's face meant she was ready to go. He put up his index finger signaling for her to wait a minute and dialed the connect.

"Hello", a deep voice answered.
"What's good? This Real…"

The deep voice interrupted. "Hold up! Meet me at the address she gave you in a hour." CLICK!

Real had a puzzled look on his face, until it dawned on him that he was talking too reckless on the phone! He went to his sister's apartment and grabbed all of the money he stacked, then made his way back to the

Cadillac. Real was completely baffled as Dynasty drove up the high hill and parked at the address China Doll had given him. It was a beat up dusty looking barn yard surrounded by a field full of tall grass.

"Where the hell he at?" Real wondered as his eyes scanned the area.

Dynasty shrugged her shoulders.

"He's probably inside."

Real knew Benji wouldn't put him in harm's way, but just to be on the safe side, he cocked back his black .9 mm before getting out of the car and began walking to the barn.

He slowly opened the barn door, and as he peeked inside he saw an older well dressed bald head man who stood on the opposite side with his back against the wall and arms folded across his chest. He wore a tailored Prada suit with a red tie, and hard bottom Prada shoes. "Lock the door behind you."

Real closed the door and locked it. The man noticed the gun that Real tucked away, but paid it no mind. "I'm All Things", he stated firmly introducing himself.

All Things was the invisible hand that supplied majority of the state of New Jersey with the purest cocaine. He was never seen nor heard. Only the elite were blessed with the privilege to be in his presence. All Things had the man power to design the underworld however he wanted it, and was politically connected which made him a very powerful man.

"I could tell by the way you talked over the phone you're not aware of how we must conduct ourselves in this life that chose us."
"Nah, Benji put me up on game. I was just kind of anxious to finally get plugged in, that's all."

All Things wasn't trying to hear it. "If it happens again, I'll be forced to cut our ties", he said seriously.

Real nodded his head, "Yeah, I understand. It won't happen again" he replied respectfully.

"I'll be right back, I'm about to go grab the money real quick."
"There's no need to do that. In this field you must keep your hands as clean as possible. If you're anything like Benji, in the near future you will have your own empire, and will be too important to jeopardize your freedom. Oh yeah, however many keys you buy, you will receive that same amount on consignment."

All Things smirked, noticing the way Real's eyes grew wide.
"I will have my people call you in exactly one week from now at 5 o'clock in the evening."
"Aight."

Real exited the barn and climbed back inside of his Cadillac.
"Damn! It took you long enough!" Dynasty said with an attitude. "If I would've kept the car running we would've been sitting here on E!"

"Man, you the one who said I can't go nowhere without you. Don't cry now."

I gotta hurry up and learn how to drive so I could roll dolo! I can't argue and handle business at the same time, Real thought shaking his head.

"So what happened? Why you ain't come get the money?" Dynasty asked.
"Because he told me to hold everything, and that his peoples will call me in a week to let me know what's up."

Dynasty sucked her teeth.
"So you mean to tell me that I drove way out here for nothing?"
"We ain't come out here for nothing. We set everything up so shit can run smooth", Real shot back.

Dynasty sighed out loud, obviously frustrated. *I ain't gon' be going through this dumb shit,* she thought to herself as she started the car up and pulled off.

For the next two weeks, Dynasty taught Real how to drive, and Real taught Dynasty how to shoot. They were too young to go to the shooting range to practice so they went to the park at 4am every morning and shot at the glass bottles they placed on the bleachers for target practice. The first time Dynasty let off a shot, the loud sound and impact scared her to the point she dropped the gun and started running. Real couldn't help but to laugh. As the days went by, she was able to get the hang of it.

Real was a fast learner, so he pretty much had the fundamentals of driving down at the end of the first week. His only problem was that he had a habit of using two feet while driving.

Real cruised up Southard Street and made a right turn on the Boulevard.

"See, you doing it again!" Dynasty said looking down at Real's feet.

Real's left foot was pressed down on the brake pedal and his right foot rested on the gas.

"No I'm not", he argued as he quickly removed his left foot.

"Yeah whatever boy! I just saw you move your foot."

Real smirked as he looked at his watch. It read 4:59pm.

"Oh shit, it's 5 o'clock."

As soon as he finished his sentence, he felt his phone vibrating.

"Yo", Real answered.

"Meet me in the laundromat on Brunswick with the dirty laundry in five minutes", a female ordered with a heavy Spanish accent before hanging up in his ear.

Five minutes was more than enough time. He went to his home to grab his small duffle bag filled with cash from out of the closet, and then made his way to the laundromat.

Dynasty stayed in the car while Real left with the duffle bag and walked through the medium sized parking lot. When Real stepped through the glass door he spotted an exotic looking Latina behind the counter staring at him. The woman gave him a sexy smile as she nodded her head indicating that she was the one that called him. Real approached her placing the duffle bag on the counter.

"That's 45 large right there."

Without saying a word, she picked the bag up and disappeared behind the clothes. Within minutes she appeared in front of the counter with a note in her hand. She held it up to Real's face.

Go to the car wash on Chambers and get your car washed now. You will get your money's worth.

After Real read the note the woman ripped it into tiny pieces and threw it away.

Real drove to the car wash on Chambers Street where three men were standing by. Two of them held cleaning supplies, while the other man waved his hand, motioning for Real to drive towards him. Real parked the

Cadillac in front of the men. One of them tapped on the window.

"Get out the car so we can clean it."

Real and Dynasty got out of the car and watched them as they cleaned the car inside out. Minutes later, they were done and the Cadillac was spotless. One of the men approached Real and Dynasty and said, "It's in the trunk."

Dynasty and Real were amazed at how All Things maneuvered his illegal business through his legal business. Real nodded his head.

"Aight", he stated before pulling a $20 dollar bill out of his pocket to pay for the cleaning.

Real and Dynasty got in the clean Cadillac and pulled off.

CHAPTER 5

After the the car wash, Real and Dynasty went straight to the trap house and went to work. The six keys of coke were so pure, Real stretched it to twelve keys and it still came back decent. Real taught Dynasty everything there was to know about coke and a scale. When they finished weighing and bagging, Real texted Dose and Snake Eyes letting them know that everything was back in motion.

Neither of them saw Real since his release, so they texted him back immediately letting him know they wanted to meet up ASAP. Real responded telling them to meet him in front of the projects.

Dynasty carried the gym bag as they walked in Tadasia's apartment. Tadasia was sitting on the living room couch.
"Lil brother guess what."
"What happened?" Real asked with raised eyebrows as he approached his big sister.
"I'm about to buy a house."

"Word up?" Real exclaimed hugging his big sister as tight as he could.

Tadasia was what you called a strong, black independent woman that went hard for hers. She bust her ass working two jobs 6 days a week, and for a side hustle she exploited her good credit by renting expensive cars for all the drug dealers in the area and over charging them.

Real was so happy that Tadasia finally had an opportunity to leave the raggedy projects. He was at a loss for words and all he could do was smile and continue to hold her. Dynasty stood there watching the two enjoy their special little moment.

"So when are you supposed to be moving?"
"In 2 or 3 weeks. You gon' like it too. It's nice and there's a lot of room."

Real suddenly felt his cell phone vibrating. When he pulled out his phone he saw that it was a text from Dose.
IM IN FRONT OF THE BUILDING.

"Hold on big sis. I'll be right back. I got to go handle something", Real told her before he rushed out of the front door.

When Real stepped out of Tadasia's building he saw Dose sitting on the bench.
"What's good my nigga?"

Dose greeted and slapped hands with Real.

"You already fucking know, that paper spread. Come in the hallway", Real responded.
"Man these niggas out here scared to death now that you home."
"Why you say that?"
"I don't know how Roe knew you were home, but he came up to me the other day and told me to tell you that he don't want any problems and all this other sucker shit."
"Oh, yeah?"

That fat fuck head probably scared as hell! I could use him for something. All I got to do is feed him with a long spoon, Real said to himself.

For the next 20 minutes Dose informed Real on everything that went on in the 'hood during his brief incarceration. When Dose was finished, Real placed both of his hands on his shoulders and looked him dead in the eyes.

"Listen, from here on out if the work ain't coming from us it can't be sold around here. I also want all the sales to be served inside the hallway, and I want you to deal with Roe fat ass from now on. I don't want him too close to me, nah mean. So when you see him tell him what this new movement be 'bout, and tell him no matter how big I can cover the order.""

Dose nodded his head in agreement.
"Aight my nigga, I got you."
"Hold on real quick."

Real went in to his sister's apartment and within seconds came out carrying a black plastic bag with two kilos inside it.
"That's two of them thangs."

Real handed Dose the black bag.
"You can handle that, right?"
"Yeah, I got it. I'll see you when I'm done," Dose replied making his way down the stairwell.

Despite what Benji thought of him, Real knew Dose would be the perfect nigga for the job. He never showed any traits of being a slime ball, his clientele was out of this world, and everyone in the 'hood had love for him. He was a good dude all around the board.

Real and Dynasty were in the hallway on the second floor looking out the window waiting for Snake Eyes to come through.
"That must be them right there", Real said noticing a black Buick with dark tints slowly pull up in front of the building.

Real cocked back his black .9mm before tucking it in his front hoodie pocket. Dynasty held a chrome .38 revolver in her small hand.
"If you see anything funny come down squeezing."

Real walked down the stairway.

Although business was business, the last thing Real was going to let happen was for him to get caught slipping. He had to be very cautious when dealing with Snake Eyes because the young thug Ricky, that Kaze bodied, was from his 'hood.

Snake Eyes got out of the passenger seat of the Buick when he saw Real standing there with his hand in his hoodie pocket. Real slowly backed up in to the hallway.
"Who that driving?"

Snake Eyes noticed the intensity in Real's movements and immediately knew what it was about.
"I ain't got nothing to do with that shit you and them li'l niggas from my 'hood going through!"

Snake Eyes lifted his shirt up to show Real that he didn't have a pistol on him.

"That's my righthand man Low Down driving. We ain't come out here on no bullshit! We came out here to handle business."

Real eased up and removed his hand from out of his hoodie pocket.
"Come in the hallway. I just…"
"That shit ain't 'bout nothing. Let me get four of them thangs."

If this li'l shithead nigga can serve me four birds, that meant Benji left him the plug, Snake Eyes thought to himself enviously.

"Where the money at?" Real asked.

Um hum, just like I thought, Snake Eyes thought.
"It's in the car, I'm about to go grab it."

Snake Eyes went to the car, grabbed the duffle bag filled with cash out of the trunk, and walked back into the hallway.
"That's 50 large right there."

Real frowned.

"Where the other fifty at?"
"Damn man! I ain't have to spend no money when my nigga Benji was home, you could at least front me what I spend. I'm trying to eat too!"

Snake Eyes was a good fast talker. Real let out a deep breath, and looked up at the ceiling.
"Aight man, wait right here."

Real ran up the stairwell with the bag of money. Seconds later, he came back down, served Snake Eyes and sent him on his way.

Within a few days, Real had moved eight keys of coke as if they were only eight ounces and was already on his way to the laundromat to re-up. He made a vow to himself that he would flip his whole had the next 10 times he went to re-up. Each time it was the same procedure, Real dropped the bread off at the laundromat then picked up the coke from the car wash. Now that he had the plug there was no turning back, it was all or nothing.

Dynasty pulled up and parked in front of the project building with Real in the passenger seat. They immediately noticed Omar sitting on the bench with what appeared to be trash bags of clothes.

"I thought Tadasia said she was moving in a few weeks", Real observed as he grabbed his duffle bag from the backseat.

"She did say that", Dynasty agreed.

They approached Omar.

"What happened?" Real asked.

"Tadasia kicked me out because I told her she got to wait another two weeks before I'm able to buy furniture for the house", Omar mumbled sadly looking down at the ground.

Omar sounded just as dumb as he looked. Dynasty bust out laughing before she rushed inside the building and up the stairwell. Real frowned his face in disgust. *Man, this nigga a fucking sucker. You can't be serious,* he thought.

"Man come upstairs", Real demanded knowing how his sister could be at times, especially when she didn't get her way.

Real walked Omar upstairs where Dynasty and Tadasia were standing in the living room laughing. Tadasia saw Omar walking behind Real.

"Get the fuck out of my house!"

"Chill out and get off your bullshit Tadasia", Real said.

"I don't want to hear shit! His lying ass should've bought my furniture today!"

Real's facial expression read, *Come on now, if you don't knock it off!*

"He said he's going to get all the furniture next week. You don't move for two weeks anyway. Damn! Let him live a little bit!"

Tadasia calmed down to listen to what her brother was saying, and realized she was being stubborn . She glanced over at Dynasty and smirked.

"Alright, he can stay here but his ass sleeping right on the couch!"

Tadasia stormed into her room and slammed the door.

"Good looking li'l bro!" Omar said feeling relieved.

"You better hurry up and go get your clothes before somebody steal them", Real warned.

Omar rushed out of the apartment. Dynasty laughed as he ran down the stairs.

"That shit ain't funny", Real said.

"Oh yes it is!"

I don't care how much money a broad got, nor how good she look, I'll never be on some sucker shit like that! Real thought to himself shaking his head. He went into his room and stashed the duffle bag under his bed.

RING! RING! RING! Real heard the cordless phone ringing and strolled back into the living room. By then Dynasty already answered it, and was talking to whoever it was that called.

"Who that?" Real asked approaching Dynasty, who was now seated on the couch with the phone to her ear.

"Here he go right here", Dynasty said smiling handing Real the phone.

"Hello?"

"Hey son. How are you?"

Nyla called at least once a week to check up on her kids. Real's face lit up when he heard his mother's voice.

"What's up mom? I'm doing good, how about you?"

Just hearing her children's voice gave Nyla strength. She stayed clean since the drug program, and was determined to come home and do the right thing.

"I'm doing swell. Your girlfriend sounds like she's nice. I can't wait to meet her."

"Yeah mom, she's shot all the way out, you're going to love her."

Dynasty playfully punched Real in the arm.

"Don't be telling her that."

"So how are you doing in school?" Nyla asked.

"I'm doing aight", Real lied.

Real had dropped out of school, the only time he went to school was to gamble.
"When are you coming home?" Real asked changing the subject.
"I should be home in 4-6 months. Where's Tadasia?" "She's in her room."
"I only got a few minutes left, let me talk to her real quick."
"Aight, love you mom."
"I love you too son."

Real brought the phone to Tadasia's room, "Mommy on the phone."

Tadasia took the phone and shut the door. Omar came through the door with his bags when Real walked in to the living room. He looked at Dynasty.
"I'm hungry as hell. Let's go get something to eat."

Dynasty looked at her watch.
"We better hurry up and go because Kaze's visit start at 3 o'clock and it's 2:15."

The couple rushed out of the door.

"Welcome to KFC, may I take your order please", the female voice said on the drive thru intercom.

"Yeah, um...let me get 8 pieces of boneless barbecue chicken and 4 biscuits" Real ordered leaning over Dynasty so she could hear him clearly.

"Okay, pull up front."

When Dynasty pulled up to pay, Real noticed Snake Eyes' Buick pulling up in the parking lot. *Oh shit. What them hoes doing driving Snake Eye's car?* Real wondered surprised when he saw Kia and Tia get out and strut inside.

Dynasty got the food and pulled out. She drove to pick up Qadeesha before taking Real to go visit his brother from another mother. The only reason Dynasty went to go pick up Qadeesha was to keep her company while she waited during the visit.

As soon as Real stepped foot in the crowded visiting hall, his eyes scanned through the people that sat in rows of chairs and spotted Kaze in the corner on the right. Kaze smiled and nodded his head. Real smiled back walking towards him. They hadn't seen each other ever since the day Kaze took the charge, so they both were kind of excited about the visit.

"What's good bruh?" Kaze greeted standing up slapping hands with Real.

Kaze had his hair in box braids and wore a tan khaki button up shirt with the pants to match. They sat across from each other.

"You already know I'm making it happen. The 'hood miss you though."
"Oh yeah? How everything moving out there?"
"How ever we want it to move. Niggas can't sell a crumb of coke in the 'hood if it ain't coming from us."
"Word up?! Benji gave you the plug?"
"Hell yeah."

"Word up!"

"Guess who tried to come and cop the fifth as soon as I came home."

"Who?"

"Roe bitch ass, that's who!"

"Man, don't trust that nigga", Kaze warned.

"Oh you ain't got to worry. I don't play that fuckboy close. I let Dose deal with him", Real explained before looking around the visiting hall.

"What's going on in here, it look like you losing weight. Let me find out you getting ya trays took from you in here", Real said jokingly.

"Yeah, aight. I got this shit on smash and I ain't even been down here a whole month yet."

"Oh, right before I came here to see you I saw Tia and Kia at the KFC."

"Oh yeah. That bitch just wrote me out of the blue a few days ago, talking about she forgive me and all this other groupie shit. I'm gon' write her back tonight. You know a nigga need as many broads I can get on the team while I'm doing the time."

Real nodded his head in agreement. After the 30 minute visit, Real put a few grand on Kaze's books and he and the ladies headed home.

CHAPTER 6

So much had gone on within the past four years it was ridiculous! Real had majority of Trenton on smash as far as the coke game was concerned. Instead of eliminating the competition with violent behavior, Real put his crafty hustling skills to use by lowering the prices and supplying better product, cornering the market.

During his ambitious climb to the top All Things took a very serious liking to him and become his mentor, bringing out his full potential. The life of a full blown boss couldn't have been better for Real. He had all the money he could dream of, and he made sure everyone from his squad was eating. In return they showed him unconditional love and loyalty.

After being released from rehab, his mother stayed clean and sober. Real put her in a big green and white house with a picket fence in the suburbs. He also invested in a lucrative beauty salon and put it in his sister's name.

The love of his life, Dynasty, was pregnant with their first child, a baby girl. The only person missing was Kaze.

During Kaze's incarceration, Real made sure he lived like a king. He kept money stacked on his books, sent him tons of pictures, and made sure Qadeesha and his mother was straight. Carla also moved into a big house in the suburbs and didn't want for nothing. Real also looked out for Benji, who was in the Feds doing a 10 year bid. Many dudes in the 'hood talked that real shit, but Real was living it.

Dynasty was half sleep in their king sized bed when she went to wrap her arm around Real. Her eyes suddenly popped open when she felt nothing but an empty space. She quickly sat up, and noticed that he was near the closet hurriedly putting on his clothes. "Where the hell you think you going?" Dynasty asked him.

Damn man! Real silently cursed as he slipped into his black and blue Gucci sneakers. He was trying to make it out the house before Dynasty woke up but failed terribly.

"I'm about to go out and handle some business."

"Hold on. I'm coming too."

The little bubble that poked through Dynasty's sheer lingerie hinted she was a few months pregnant.

"No you not!" Real firmly told her while watching her slip into her True Religion pants.

"Oh yes I am!"

"No you not. You got my mufucking child in your stomach."

Dynasty sucked her teeth as Real began walking towards her.

"You can't be running the streets with me how you used to. If some shit pop off then what?"

Dynasty just stood there without saying a word.

"That's what I thought. From this day on, ya ass about to start doing what baby mommas do and that's take care of home."

Dynasty placed her arms across her chest and poked her lips out. She was pissed off. The logic behind Real's words made it impossible for her to argue against what he said.
"I don't want to be sitting in the house all day by myself", she whined.

Feeling relieved, Real slightly smirked. He thought he was going to be arguing with Dynasty for at least an hour.
"You ain't got to stay here. I'm gonna drop you off at my mom spot so you could chill with her. You know how y'all do."

Dynasty smiled knowing whenever she and Nyla got together they had fun and bugged out to the fullest. Throughout the years they had developed an amazing mother/daughter relationship. If Dynasty and Real got into their little beefs, Nyla would always side with Dynasty over her son.

Real climbed out of his tented out triple black Aston Martin Vanquish. The delicious aroma of cookout food crept into his nostrils and he heard Marvin Gaye's *"Sexual Healing"* coming from his mother's backyard. *Mommy back there cooking on the grill,* Real thought as he went over to the passenger door opening it for Dynasty.

"Damn that food smells good as hell!" Dynasty said.

"I know, right?"

Real gently grabbed her by the hand and led her through the side of the house. There they saw Nyla standing over top of the smoking grill with a big fork in her hand turning the barbecue ribs. She wore a colorful flower print dress with matching sandals, and a straw hat that blocked her face from the bright sun. Nyla saw them coming.

"There go my son and my two li'l mommas!" Nyla said excitedly as she placed her fork on the wooden table near the grill. "Y'all just in time! The food is almost finished."

Nyla lowered her head near Dynasty's stomach.

"And I know my granddaughter hungry, ain't she?" She said in a playful baby voice. "Don't worry, grandma gon' fix you a nice big plate."

Dynasty blushed while Real smiled shaking his head. It seemed as though Nyla was more excited about the baby coming into the world, than Dynasty and Real was. Dynasty was no where near her due date, and Nyla had already bought tons of clothes and toys for her unborn grandchild.

"What you gonna do? Just stand there boy? Give ya mom a hug!"

Nyla opened her arms. Real gave his mother a huge hug.

"Boy you're looking more and more like your dad as the years pass."

Nyla never lied! At the age of 17 Real's lean frame stood 6' 3" and his jet black wavy hair and million dollar smile made his shiny chocolate skin appear flawless. The mentioning of his father stung his heart, and caused unusual emotions to travel through his body. Although he didn't know his father he still loved him dearly. He loved the memory of him, but at the same time felt resentment for him not being in his life.

Nyla noticed the look in her son's eyes and quickly switched the subject.
"Now y'all go grab a seat. I'm about to fix y'all a plate."

Nyla grabbed the fork from off the wooden table.

"Mom, I gotta go handle some important business. I just stopped by to drop Dynasty off because she ain't want to stay in the house by herself", Real said.

This boy can never just sit still! Nyla thought to herself shaking her head from side to side.
"Well, you could at least take something to eat with you."

Nyla quickly made Real's plate and handed it to him.

"Aight, I'll see you lovely ladies when I get back."

Real kissed Dynasty and Nyla on the check and began munching down on a rib while exiting the backyard.

As soon as Real stepped foot inside of the barn All Things was there waiting.
"What took you so long?"

All Things was standing a few feet away from the door. He wore a simple white tank top to match his white Air Force sneakers, and some grey Polo sweatpants. All Things usually wore dress shirts and hard bottoms, so to see him dressed so simply was kind of shocking to Real.

"My baby mom got on some bullshit because I wouldn't let her come with me and we started arguing so I dropped her off at my mom's. She ain't want to stay in the crib by herself."

Real and All Things slapped hands and embraced.

"You got a lot on ya hands, huh?" All Things smirked.

"Yeah, something like that. So what did you have to show me?"

"I needed you to take care of something for me but it's already handled, so no need to mention it. I want to show you my house."

Real looked puzzled.

"So why you choose to meet up here?"

All Things chuckled and pressed a button on his iced out custom made Rolex watch. Real's eyes grew wide when he noticed the hidden door in the center of the barn floor slowly slide open. Real was amazed. He had only seen shit like that on TV. Throughout the years, he always wondered where in the hell All Things disappeared to in this particular spot, there was never a car anywhere in sight! All Things never left the barn with Real.

"This is the way to my house."

All Things led Real down the stairs to an underground tunnel. Once they made it to the bottom of the steps, All Things pressed another button on his Rolex, closing the hidden door. A four-wheeler was parked waiting.
"Get on the back."

Real hopped on and All Things sped off through the long underground tunnel. It took 10 minutes to reach the end which led to another stairwell. All Things threw the four-wheeler in park. Another hidden door dropped down to reveal stairs. The stairs led to an all black spacious room containing an arsenal. Every machine gun you could possibly think of hung from the ceiling. There was a fancy black desk and a chair in the right corner where computer monitors surveilled every room of his mini mansion and also showed the barnyard. *Who the fuck this nigga think he is? Black Scarface?!* Real thought in amazement as his eyes scanned the room.

All Things closed the hidden door.

"This is the war room. I spend most of my time in here thinking and strategizing. But this ain't a time for war, it's a time to enjoy ourselves. Since this is your first time here, let me show you around. Come on."

All Things opened the door to the next room. As soon as he stepped foot inside Real thought he was in Hawaii or Tahiti some where! There were giant palm trees, a see through king size water bed with colorful fish swimming inside, and in the middle of the room, colorful rocks and tropical flowers decorated the Jacuzzi which gave it a unique forest lake view.

"I'm sure you can pretty much figure out what goes on in this room", All Things chuckled opening the door which lead to the next room.

Real was speechless as he looked around, still following All Things. It seemed like every room held a theme more surprising than the next. They finally ended up in the game room at the mini bar just off the kitchen. There was a pool table in the middle of the floor and a juke box near the sliding glass doors, which led to the enormous backyard.

"What you drinking?" All Things asked as he walked behind the bar.
"Henny", Real replied as he sat on the stool.

All Things grabbed a bottle of Henny and two double shot glasses out of the cabinet and poured Real and himself something to drink. They both threw the shots back like it was water. All Things poured anther round. Real could hear female voices coming from the backyard. He saw three exotic looking Latinas wearing bikinis entering through the glass sliding doors. They had just gotten out of the pool so their voluptuous bodies were glistening from the water. Real's lustful eyes stared at the three beautiful women. He turned back to All Things who had a smirk on his face.
"I know you didn't think I was living in this big ass house all alone."

Real could do nothing but shake his head.

"Damn daddy, why you ain't let us know you were back?" The bronze Dominican asked as she strutted towards All Things.

Real watched as her booty jiggled with every step she took.

"I haven't even been back 5 minutes yet", All Things responded.

She approached him and grabbed his manhood.
"After we're done cleaning, we want to have a session in the pool", she whispered in All Things' ear before licking his neck.

All Things kissed her on the lips as he palmed her ass cheeks.
"Don't you see we got company? Stop being rude and introduce yourself", he said smoothly before smacking her ass causing it to jiggle.

All three women looked at each other and giggled. While everyone began introducing themselves All Things went over to the jukebox to turn on some music, getting the party going. They started a pool tournament, drunk until they couldn't drink anymore, laughed, joked and danced all night long.

CHAPTER 7

They day of Kaze's return had finally come and Real had everything lined up and in order. He couldn't wait to see his brother set free from confinement and back to the real world so he could rule the streets along with him and Dose, who had proven to be extremely loyal over the years. Real bought Kaze a gun smoke grey LS 460 Lexus, three sets of jewelry, twin gold 40 caliber handguns with pearl handles, along with 250 grand as coming home presents. Real told himself once Kaze was released and learned the way things were moving, he would fall back and let him run everything so he could spend majority of his time with Dynasty raising their daughter.

It was a bright and sunny morning. Real was driving down the Boulevard in his Aston Martin with the top down. He had dropped Dose off in the projects and was now on his way to China Doll's house to grab a letter that Benji wrote him. Real smirked when he noticed the principal of the school he dropped out of parking his car across the street from the school. He looked at his iced out Rolex which read 10:30am. *This fuck head must be coming from his break,* Real said to himself pulling up closely along side of his car, damn near running the principal over.

Real slammed his foot on the brake pedal causing the tires to screech. Frightened and caught by surprise, the principal almost jumped out of his skin! He had to jump backward against his car door to prevent from being hit by the Aston Martin. Real saw the terrified look on the old man's face and chuckled.

"Remember me mufucka? You told me that I'll be dead or in jail before I'm 18. Look at me now! I'm alive and I got more money than ya old ass!"

Real pulled out a wad of cash from his pocket and threw it in the old man's face before speeding off down the street.

KNOCK! KNOCK! KNOCK! "Who is it?" China Doll asked peeping through the door.
"It's Real."

China Doll took the lock off and opened the door for Real to come in. She began walking towards the kitchen. When Real stepped inside he couldn't help but notice her ample behind jiggling in her pink booty shorts. He tried his best not to look but couldn't help it. He constantly glanced at the spectacular view as he followed her to the kitchen.

China Doll grabbed Benji's letter off the refrigerator and handed it to Real. He grabbed the letter trying his best not to look at her erect nipples poking through her tank top. China Doll noticed how Real was avoiding looking at her and sucked her teeth.

"Boy you act like you ain't never seen ass and titties before."

Yeah I seen 'em, but not like yours!, Real said to himself. He ripped the envelope, took the letter out, and began reading it.

> **Li'l Bro, what's good? I'm going to try to keep this short and simple. I need you now more than ever. I'm about to get moved to Mercer County. The State just**

hit me with a murder charge and from the way they talking it sounds like they got some hardcore evidence on ya boy. I only got 20k and the lawyer I need to spank the case is 80k. If you can make something happen for me, make it happen!

Damn! They trying to bury big bro alive, Real sadly thought, looking at China Doll who stood in front of him licking her pink full lips. She looked down and noticed the bulge in Real's sweats. Knowing she had Real aroused, a naughty little grin appeared on her face as she dug her hand into his sweatpants touching his thickness. She stuck her tongue in his mouth and started kissing him.

China Doll loved Benji and held it down as long as she could, but when that murder charge popped up she started considering other options. She felt he may never be coming home and decided to move on to the next fly boss to keep her in the lifestyle she had grown accustomed to.

A low grunt escaped Real's mouth and his eyes rolled behind his head as China Doll dropped down to her knees and pulled Real's sweats all the way down with one hand still attending to his throbbing dick with the other. She was turned on at the sight of his king sized snicker and couldn't wait to taste him. China Doll's intention was to suck him and fuck him until he was strung out, giving her any and everything she wanted.

As China Doll went to put his manhood in her mouth, Real broke out of his trance and realized the reality of what was about to take place. He quickly pushed her head back and took a few steps backwards.
"I can't do my big bruh like this", Real said out loud while pulling up his Gucci sweats.

The head in his pants told him to continue, but the head on his shoulders reminded him that Benji was the one that introduced him to the game and to cross him by fucking his main lady would be the ultimate betrayal.

"What the fuck you mean you can't do this?!"

China Doll got up from her knees and looked at Real like he was insane. She was devastated. Not once in her whole entire life had a man turned her down.

"Nigga, you don't see all this?" She said arrogantly slipping out of the pink shorts with her hand on her hip.

China Doll had the body of a goddess, and she didn't have one blemish on her soft yellow skin. Real's eyes looked like they were going to pop out of his head when he looked down and saw China Doll's glistening camel toe. She noticed the shocking lust in Real's eyes. *I got his li'l young ass right where I want him,* she said to herself walking over to get the pink dildo out of the drawer near the sink.

"You scared of this good wet pussy ain't you?" She asked reclining on the kitchen table lifting her pretty little foot in the air and placing it on the chair.

China Doll slid the dildo insider her wetness, and began popping herself.

"Aaaaw yeah! You see how wet this pussy get?"

China Doll moaned and looked at Real while moving the dildo in and out of her neatly shaven soaking wet pussy. Thick creamy juices flowed down the dildo on to her well manicured hand.
"Oh shit, I'm cumming!"

Man, let me get the hell out of this house before I end up fucking this bitch, Real said to himself. He darted out of the kitchen and out the front door.

Max B's *"I'm a Million Dollar Baby"* blared through Real's speakers as he pulled up in the projects. He looked around and smirked at how live his 'hood was. A group of young girls were playing double dutch near the park where another group of little kids were running around having fun. Several young hustlers from Real's squad stood around a couple of young women that were half dressed, exposing their voluptuous bodies.

They were popping jokes on each other making the young ladies laugh.

Leaving the car running and music playing loudly, Real climbed out looking for Dose. *Where the fuck this nigga at?* He said to himself. He passed by two old heads that were sitting on the hood of a green Taurus.

"What's good Real?" One greeted as Real approached them.

"What's up. Y'all seen Dose out here?"

"He around here somewhere. I just saw him", the other said.

Real had come to pick Dose up so they could meet up with Kaze at Qadeesha's to take him shopping. He looked near the playground and spotted a crowd of people shooting dice. He looked at his watch, it read 12:30pm. *I got just enough time to stick these niggas real quick,* Real said to himself as he walked over to the dice game. He figured if Dose wasn't around after a while he would leave him.

"Man I'm grabbing bank", Real stated like a boss as he slid through the crowd of men standing around.

Real pulled a wad of cash out of his pocket. The old head that shook the dice was just about to role them against the red brick wall, but stopped when he heard what Real said.
"Li'l nigga, you can't just come over here talking about you grabbing bank! You know what you got to roll on them dice to do that."

Everybody knew the old head as X. He was tall and light skin with long dreads. He used to do it real big back in the day but was now washed up, still trying to live up to who he used to be. He had a little bit of money, but was nowhere near Real's level, which made him envious.

The group of gamblers that stood on the sideline talking slick to one another immediately got quiet, knowing that X's hostile attitude could cost him more than he could afford. Real took X's words offensively and looked at him like he had lost his mind.

"Old timer, don't you ever li'l nigga me! I got piles of money sitting in my stash house bigger than you."

X threw the dice against the red brick wall and rolled craps, 1 2 3. Real chuckled as he picked the dice up from the ground.
"What's the fade?"
"A hundred", one of the young men on the sideline said.
"That's it?" Real hollered with a lifted eyebrow looking at X standing on the opposite side.
"Alright li'l man, lay 10 racks to my 15. I'll shoot star or better!" X said sarcastically.

Real dropped $10 grand on the ground. X knew damn well he didn't have it like that to be placing all that money on one shot, but he did it anyway just to prove a point.
"It's a bet", he said.

X pulled out $15 grand dropped and placed it on the ground. Everyone'e eyes were on Real as he shook the dice and threw them against the wall, rolling 4 5 6.

"Like I said, I got bank", Real taunted X as he kneeled down and picked his winnings up from the ground.

Real stood up to count his winnings. He then looked at everyone in the crowd.
"It can't be nothing less than five hundred down in ya bank, so if ya paper ain't long, go play in traffic."

Real's intent was to get to $50 grand as quickly as possible then go meet up with his brother from another mother. He smirked at the stupid look on X's face then picked up the dice again and began shaking them.
"What's up? You laying 15 racks again or what?"
"Yeah, I'll lay it again. That shit ain't about nothing!" X replied.

Meanwhile, Kaze was smiling uncontrollably as he followed the correctional officer that was assigned to escort him off the premises. He carried a bag filled with his pictures and mail. The CO took his walkie talkie from off his belt and put it up to his mouth.

"Open Gate 3."

Kaze looked up at the clear blue sky and let out a loud sigh of relief. *This shit is finally over*, he said to himself. The energy that traveled through his body was indescribable as the metal gate slowly opened. During his time all he did was plan, plan and plan some more. Now the time was finally here to put everything in to play.

"Kaze go home and stay home. I don't want to see you walking back through these doors", the CO said.

This cop ass mufucka don't give a fuck about me, Kaze thought.
"I'd rather die than come back in here", he responded harshly before walking out of the gate.

Kaze was wild and crazy as hell, but he was no fool. He did his time peacefully and away from any trouble. His main goal was to make his first eligibility date and he did it. Kaze scoped out the parking lot and spotted

Qadeesha standing in front of her black Benz truck. Rays from the sun beamed down on her shiny golden skin. Her short sleeve Prada shirt paralleled the gray and blue Prada skirt she wore that stopped mid thigh. Her open toed Prada sandals exposed her well manicured toes.

"Baby!" Qadeesha exclaimed joyfully as she ran to Kaze with open arms.

Kaze quickly dropped his bag and took her into his embrace.

"I'm so happy that you're finally home!" Qadeesha yelled holding him tightly as if she never wanted to let him go.

Without missing a beat she rode the whole bid out with Kaze and was now about to be rewarded for her loyalty. Little did she know Kaze had plans to propose. Qadeesha's sweet scent and soft touch caused Kaze's manhood to rise immediately. Without saying a word he began kissing her passionately. Their hands explored each other's bodies. The two finally caught their composure, Kaze picked up his bag.

"Come on", he whispered, gently grabbing her by the hand and leading her to the car.

Once they got into the car Kaze was like a dog in heat! He ripped off his tan khaki shirt and began licking and sucking on Qadeesha's thighs while trying to lift up her skirt.

"Damn, baby you're going to get some. Wait until we get home."

Qadeesha struggled to remove Kaze's head from between her thick thighs.

"Mmm..., I want it now!" He lustfully begged as he tried to remove her hands.

"Boy I'm not fucking you in this parking lot! You been without pussy for 4 years, you can wait until we get home!"

"Aight man, hurry up and drive."

Kaze knew he wasn't going to be able to hit it when they got home because Real and Dose were going to be there waiting for him to arrive.

"Where ya phone at?" Kaze asked.

"It's in my purse", Qadeesha said trying her best to hold her laugh in as she pulled out of the parking lot.

Kaze grabbed Qadeesha's cell phone out of her stylish Prada purse and dialed Real's number.

The enormous crowd of spectators made it seem like the entire Donnelly Homes Projects was watching as the two went head to head. Real was up $40 grand in the beginning, but the tables had turned and he was now down $80 grand. After losing all of the money in his pockets, Real made Dose, who had finally popped up, run and get a bag full of money out of one of his stash houses.

"Yo! Hold on. Stop the dice...Yo?" Real answered after putting the phone to his ear.

"What's good, bruh? Me and Qadeesha on our way to the house right now. You and Dose already there right?" Kaze asked.

"Nah, we ain't there right now."

Real looked at Dose who was standing near him on guard with his hand on his strap just in case someone tried something stupid.

"We'll be there before you and Qadeesha get there."
"Where y'all at?"
"In the 'hood gambling"
"You just can't leave them dice alone huh?"
Kaze smiled. "Well we gon' be at the house in like 25 minutes so..."

Real didn't let him finish.
"We gon' be there before then."
"You sure man? Because you know how you get with them dice!"
"Yeah, I'm sure."
"Aight then, I'll see you when I get to the crib."

The two hung up.

"Aight! Shoot the dice!" Real hollered moving aside so X can shoot the dice.

X threw the dice against the brick wall.

"Crap!" Real shouted out loud picking up the dice and his winnings in one swipe.

"That shit ain't 'bout nothing! This ya money you struggling to win back!" X shouted, getting under Real's skin.

X also had a bag filled with cash on the ground near him with one of his goons strapped up on stand by.

"This money ain't 'bout nothing to me old timer. I got enough of it to give away to the whole hood!"

"Lil nigga you can't talk to me! I was blowing money before you could blow ya own nose!" X rebutted as he turned to face Real.

While the two argued, Dose and X's gunman tensed up and ice grilled each other, waiting for someone to swing the first punch so they could start shooting shit up. Not knowing what to expect the crowd continued to watch in awe.

Meanwhile, Qadeesha pulled in front of her house and parked. Kaze surveyed the area and didn't see Real nor Dose anywhere in sight.

"Man they ain't even out here!" Kaze said picking up Qadeesha's phone.

"Roll up your window Kaze", Qadeesha demanded as she turned her car off and grabbed her purse.

While Kaze was dialing Real's number, a black Taurus with dark tinted windows slowly pulled up and stopped behind Qadeesha's truck. A masked man wearing all black hopped out of the passenger's side, gun in hand, and crept up on the passenger side.

BOOM! The masked gunman put a slug in Kaze's dome piece, causing his brain fragments to splatter all over Qadeesha's face! Terrified and in shock she screamed hysterically as the masked gunman ran off! Kaze was slumped in his seat, twitching uncontrollably while thick globs of blood oozed from his head. The sound of screeching tires could be heard as the black car sped off recklessly. Qadeesha reached down and scrambled to grab her cell phone, eventually hitting redial to call Real.

CHAPTER 8

Real and Dose rushed through the hospital door to see Kaze's mother Carla and Qadeesha standing at Kaze's bedside crying their eyes out. They turned to see Real and Dose approaching them.

"Who did this to my baby?" Carla asked as she hugged Real and began crying on his shoulder.

Real could barely look Carla in the eye as guilt consumed him. He told himself that if he would have never been gambling at that simple ass dice game, if he'd been waiting for Kaze at Qadeesha's house like he said he would, perhaps he could've prevented this tragedy.

Qadeesha was standing behind Carla. She knew exactly what Real was about to say by the way he looked at her.

"I ain't see who it was. All I saw was a black car drive off. We were just about to get out of the car and someone ran up from behind and shot him!"

Real and Carla released from each other's embrace and stood face to face.

"I don't know who did it right now but I'm going to find out!"

Real's mind was racing in a thousand different directions. He didn't have a clue on what was going on, but he was determined to get to the bottom of it. Even if it cost him his life!

Dose didn't know either of the females in the room, so he just silently stood near the door. Real looked down at Kaze and almost broke down when he saw his brother from another mother stretched out in the hospital bed with tubes going in and out of his body, and the bloody bandage covering the hole in his head. Flashbacks of the day they met when Kaze jumped in to fight Twin came to him. *Damn man! This shit mostly my fault!* Real thought as anxiety twinged his heart.

"Kaze's brain dead Real. The doctor said the only reason he's alive is because of the

machines. They're charging me $2 grand a day for medical services. I can't afford..."
"Don't worry about it. I got it", Real cut her off.

Carla inhaled then exhaled deeply.
"Thank you Real. I know you love my son as if he were your own brother so I'm going to leave the decision up to you whether or not they should pull the plug."

Real wanted to tell Carla that it wasn't for him to decide, but his words got caught in his throat. He nodded his head in agreement.
"Aight, I'm about to go out front for a li'l bit to get some fresh air and clear my mind. I'll be back", Real said.

Real placed his hands on Dose's shoulders and looked him in the eye.
"I need you to stay here and keep them company while I take a little walk and try to gather my thoughts."
"Aight my nigga", Dose agreed.

Everyone watched as Real left the hospital room. *Damn man, I can't believe this shit is happening*, he said to himself out loud as he strolled through the hospital parking lot. It was bad enough that he felt Kaze being shot was somewhat his fault, but being left with the decision to pull the plug added to the turmoil that tortured his train of thought.

Thirty minutes later, Real realized he walked down every side street off the main road of the hospital and was now on his way back. It was just beginning to get dark out, and Real was now walking down a side street full of parked cars. His phone began to vibrate. *Who the hell is this?* He thought while digging in his pocket. As soon as he put the phone to his ear several shots rang out. BLOW! BLOW! BLOW! BLOW!

A slug hit Real in the hand causing him to drop his phone to the ground.
"Ah shit!" He yelled in agony.

Real ducked behind a gray van that was parked nearby and pulled out his black 21-

shot Glock 40 from off his waistline. The blood poured from his other hand onto the pavement.

Real got to the back of the van and quickly peaked his head out to get a view of his target. He counted three masked men with their guns drawn standing side by side in the middle of the street. They began squeezing again when they saw his head pop out. BLOW! BLOW! BOW! BLOW! Several slugs hit the back of the van as Real quickly pulled his head back. *These must be the bitch ass niggas that shot Kaze,* Real thought. He felt himself begin to panic but inhaled and exhaled deeply in order to gain his composure.

Real swiftly swung half of his body from behind the van and let off several shots. BLOW! BLOW! BLOW! He hit two of the gunman in the head and upper chest before dipping back behind the van.

Fear overwhelmed the third gunman when he saw his comrades lifeless bodies fall to the ground. He began to nervously backpedal down the street with his gun still drawn. Suddenly a dark blue F150 sped around the corner at full speed crashing into the gunman, sending him flying through the air.

"Agghh!" The gunman groaned as his broken body struggled to crawl away.

Real heard the crash and poked his head out just in time to see the driver swing the door open. A slim man hopped out with a black hood over his head, walked up to the gunman, and pumped two slugs into his head. BLOW! BLOW! Real strained his eyes trying to see who the hooded man was but couldn't see clearly from his angle.

"Real! That's you my nigga?" The man yelled in Real's direction, finally removing the hood from his head.

Real smirked when he saw the man's face.

"You aight, bruh?" Snake Eyes asked looking down at Real's bleeding hand as the two approached each other.

"Yeah, I'm good! I just got hit in the hand, that's all", Real replied showing Snake Eyes the bloody gun wound.

"You gotta get to the hospital. I was riding by when I heard the shots and saw them fuck boys trying to get at you! You know..."

"Good looking out bruh, them niggas was on my ass!" Real said before Snake Eyes could finish.

"Shit it looked like you was doing aight without me! Lets hurry up and get out of here before the boys come", Snake Eyes stated urgently.

"Hell yeah, come on", Real agreed.

As they rushed to the pickup truck, Real stopped in his tracks and ran back to the gunman Snake Eyes hit with the truck. Snake Eyes watched as Real reached down to remove the mask from what was left of the dead man's bloody face.

"It was those bitch ass niggas?!" Real said in disbelief as he looked down at the familiar face.

Real recognized him as one of the thugs from the block he shot up when he came home. Snake Eyes recognized the man as well.

They heard sirens getting closer and closer so they darted to the pick-up and pulled off.

"That was li'l Daredevil from out my way", Snake Eyes exclaimed sounding just as surprised as Real.

"They had to be the bitch-ass niggas that shot Kaze", Real stated angrily as he began putting all the pieces together in the back of his mind.

Kaze killed a nigga from their 'hood, so they waited for him to come home to get at him. But why the fuck did they wait until he came home to try and get at me? And how did they know that he was coming home today?

"Kaze got shot?! I thought he was locked up!"
"He came home today. Niggas squatted on him by his crib and shot him in the head while he was getting out the car with his girl."
"Damn bruh, I'm sorry to hear that."

Snake Eyes knew that Kaze was Real's righthand man, so he couldn't imagine how he was feeling.

"Being that them fuckheads are from out my way, I'm pretty sure I can find out who was behind all this bullshit. Just give me a few days."

"If you can do that bruh, that's good looking", Real responded hoping he could really find out who targeted them.

Even though the two dealt with each other for years, Real always kept it strictly business, nothing more nothing less. But now that Snake Eyes saved his life, and was about to go out of his way to find out who was responsible for orchestrating the hit on him and Kaze, Real looked at him in a totally different light.

"Like I told you a long time ago, I don't give a fuck about them niggas from out my way when it comes to you. You the one making sure I eat out here in these streets. Just how I left that nigga in the middle of the street around the corner, I'll do the same to whoever else!" Snake Eyes emphasized every word.

They pulled up to the ER parking lot. Snake Eyes went inside the hospital with Real who received medical attention for his gunshot wound. The doctor removed the bullet, cleaned the wound, stitched him up and gave him meds. The two took the elevator to Kaze's room. Real introduced Snake Eyes to everyone and told them what had just happened.

Later that night, Real, who didn't say one word since he came inside the house, was seated on the edge of the king size bed with his shirt off staring at the wall in deep thought. Dynasty was behind him on her knees massaging his back. Real was sick to his stomach as he replayed the whole day in his mind and constantly thought about how things would've turned out if he and Dose had been at the house waiting for Kaze.

Qadeesha called and informed Dynasty about what happened, so she already knew every little detail pertaining to Kaze and could tell that Real was taking it very hard. She wanted to break the silence and ask what happened to his hand, but she told herself that she was going to wait for him to say something first. After a while her patience began to run thin.

Fuck it, I'll break the ice, she thought.
"Baby, what's going on? What happened to ya hand?" Dynasty asked in a sweet tone while still massaging his back.
"The same niggas that caught Kaze slipping tried to hit me up while I was on my way back to the hospital."
"So who was it?"
"You'll be reading about them in a few days, just pay attention to the newspaper."

Dynasty slowly shook her head, and exhaled deeply out of her nose.
"I understand Kaze's your best friend and you feel some type of way about him being shot, but you can't run around shooting shit up like it's the Wild Wild West anymore."
"I don't know why the hell I can't", Real said raising his voice.

Real couldn't believe Dynasty would say such a thing at a time like this.

"Because you got a fucking daughter on the way, that's why!" Dynasty spazzed.

The mentioning of his unborn daughter hit a nerve.

"She needs you out here Real! What if something happens to you?! You want your daughter to grow up in this cold world without her dad around to protect her, huh?!"
"Ain't nothing gon' happen to me out here!" Real attempted to calm his pregnant girl.
"How the fuck do you know?"

Dynasty got out of the bed and stood directly in front of him.
"You ain't no psychic! You can't predict the future nigga!"

Dynasty knew Real like the back of her hand, and could tell by the look on his face that he already had his mind made up.

"You so fucking selfish! All you care about is them fucking streets. Them streets don't love ya black ass, I do! Matter fact, I'm coming with you. If you riding for Kaze I'm riding too then. Fuck that!"

Dynasty knew Real wasn't going to allow that to happen, she was hoping to bend him to her will. Real stood up.
"Ya ass ain't going nowhere with my daughter in your stomach!" Real authoritatively put his foot down.
"Yes I am! You don't care so I don't care!"

The tears slid down Dynasty's soft yellow cheeks. Real was so tensed and aggravated all he could do is sit back down on the edge of the bed. He placed both of his hands on top of his head and stared down at the floor. Real knew Dynasty's feisty nature wasn't going to allow him to win their argument.

"Lets just calm down so I can gather my thoughts", he begged.
"You got enough money from off them streets. Let's just move down south near my mother

and raise our daughter in a better environment", she cried desperately.

Real remained silent for a few minutes, then looked up at Dynasty.
"You know what? You're right. I need to chill. We gon' move down south and I'm just gon' rent this house out."

Dynasty slowly closed her eyes. She inhaled and exhaled, as a feeling of relief came over her.
"So when are we leaving", she asked as she smiled looking up at Real.

She sat next to Real and wrapped her arm around his lower back.

"Right after I let my mom and sister know."

****

Nyla was in her upstairs bathroom with the door closed up to her old tricks again. She wrapped the thick rubber band around her arm, searched the inside of her forearm and spotted a worthy vein. She then grabbed her needle filled with the best heroin in the city off the floor. As she put the needle into her arm, she heard the front door open then slam shut. "Mom, where you at?!" Real yelled as he walked up the stairs.

Oh shit! Real, Nyla said to herself in a panic. She quickly snatched the rubber band off and flushed it down the toilet before stashing her needle in the cabinet under the sink.

"Mom", Real yelled again.
"I'm in the bathroom son. You screaming my name like something wrong!"

Nyla opened the bathroom door to see Real walking towards her with his hand bandaged and a depressed look on his face.
"Oh my gosh! What happened?"
"Nothing", Real replied avoiding eye contact with her.

Although Nyla was absent the majority of Real's life, she could still tell when something was bothering him.

"Let's go downstairs", she said walking towards the stairs.

Real sat down at the marble kitchen table that matched the floor. Nyla took some orange juice out of the refrigerator and poured a cup for Real and then for herself.

"Huh, baby? What's going on? Tell me what's bothering you"" she said as she handed him the cup.

Real took a sip of the cup of orange juice.

"I already told you ain't nothing wrong with me. I'm good. I got you and Tadasia some plane tickets to the Bahamas", Real told her, trying to change the subject.

Just then, they heard the front door open and close.

"You just in time", Real shouted when his big sister walked through the door.

As Tadasia strolled into the kitchen the phone began to ring. Nyla hurried over to the counter to answer.

"I'm just in time for what? I heard about what happened to Kaze. Are you alright?"

Real nodded his head and then cut his eye at his mother who was on the phone with her back turned not paying attention. He didn't tell his mother what happened because he wasn't in the mood for one of those 'what to do' and 'what not to do' speeches.

"I got you and mommy some plane tickets to go to the Bahamas for two weeks", Real said as he pulled the tickets out of his pocket.

Tadasia's eyes grew wide.
"The Bahamas!"

Real smirked at her excitement. Tadasia leaned down and gave him a hug.
"Thanks li'l bro!" She said viewing the tickets.

Real glanced at Nyla who was still on the phone. *Let me get the hell out of here before she get off the phone,* he said to himself.

"Aight, big sis, I gotta go. Love you", Real said in a low tone.

Real quickly got up from his seat, gave her a kiss on the cheek, and then darted out the house.

CHAPTER 9

Real and Dynasty secretly packed the majority of their belongings and put the 'Rent to Own' sign outside of the house. When the time came they got inside the Aston Martin and made their way down south. The long ride was tedious. Once they arrived in Greenville, South Carolina, it was late and they were both exhausted. They decided to rest at Dynasty's mother's house so they could go house shopping in the morning.

Nyla used to take Real and Tadasia to visit relatives two towns over during the summers when they were kids. It's because of this Real was somewhat familiar with the area.

"The house is right there", Dynasty said pointing at the big white and yellow house on the corner as Real drove up the dark street.

Real parked and him and Dynasty began walking towards the porch steps. All they could hear was the loud sounds of crickets coming from the tall grass in front of the house.

KNOCK! KNOCK! KNOCK! "Who is it?" A female voice yelled from behind the door.
"It's your daughter", Dynasty responded.

Real stood close beside her holding her hand.

When Dynasty's mother opened the front door she was overcome with joy.
"Oh my goodness, my baby!"

She gave her daughter a long and emotional hug.
"Why didn't you tell me you were coming down here chile?" She asked.

"Because I wanted to surprise you", Dynasty replied.

She and her mother always talked on the phone, but hadn't seen each other in over three years.

"I know that ain't what i think it is!"

A bashful smile appeared on Dynasty's face as she nodded her head and looked at Real. Dynasty's mother was so caught up and excited to see her daughter, she didn't even realize that Real was standing there. She looked over at Real and stared at him intensely as if she knew him from somewhere. "How are you doing ma'am?" Real greeted politely.

She snapped out of her trance and smiled. "You don't have to call me ma'am, my name is Tayla."

Tayla and Dynasty looked alike, but the only difference was that Tayla had a caramel complexion with light brown eyes.

"Well dag ma, can we come inside?" Dynasty joked.
"Oh shoot! Come on in!" Tayla said chuckling as she welcomed them in.

Tayla closed the door behind them.

"Make y'all selves at home."

"Oh you ain't got to worry about that, we moving down here", Dynasty informed her as her and Real sat on the long leather couch.

The couch had flower designed cushions that matched the window curtains. The living room was set up simple. There was an oval coffee table in the center of the living room, and a 42 inch flat screen tv mounted on the wall near a fish tank.

"Now chile stop fibbing", Tayla said in disbelief as she sat in her leather chair.

"I ain't lying, we're going house shopping first thing tomorrow morning. Ain't that right baby?" Dynasty nudged Real.

"Yeah."

A wide smile appeared on Tayla's face.

"You got tired of that little ole city, huh?"

"Yeah, it's too much nonsense going on and I ain't trying to raise my daughter around that."

"I know that's right. When your brother finds out you moving down here, he gon' be so happy."

She ain't never tell me she had a brother, Real thought as he looked at Dynasty.

A few hours had passed by. Real fell asleep on the couch while Dynasty and her mother stayed up all night talking about everything they could possibly think of.

During the time they spent house shopping Real and Dynasty saw many homes that appealed to them. They finally settled on a nice brick house with a large front and backyard that was down the street from Tayla's. They furnished their new home from top to bottom. Dynasty made sure that every room in her new home looked like a page from a home decor magazine. Her and Real took special care with their baby girl's nursery, making sure her room had everything she could possible want and need.

Real called Carla to check up on Kaze and immediately became depressed after she told him his condition was still the same and that nothing changed. He also called Snake Eyes, but didn't get an answer.

Dynasty relaxed on the couch with her pretty little feet resting on Real's lap enjoying a foot massage while watching *Friday After Next* on the 50 inch flat screen.. Her feet and ankles were a little swollen from all that shopping. The way Real's strong hands gently rubbed her feet began to make her honey pot heat up. "Umm baby stop rubbing my feet like that, you getting me horny", Dynasty moaned twinkling her toes.

Real's manhood grew hard just from the sound of her sexy voice. He saw the naughty look in her eyes and knew exactly what she wanted. He licked his full lips as his hands began caressing her calves working his way up to her inner thigh. Low moans escaped her lips as she slowly spread her legs. Real turned is body and lowered his head between her legs and began licking and sucking on her inner thigh.

"Shit", Dynasty moaned as she closed her eyes and grabbed the back of Real's head.

KNOCK! KNOCK! KNOCK! Suddenly someone knocked on the door. Dynasty sucked her teeth. Real sat up and went to answer the door. He knew that it couldn't have been anyone but Tayla or Dynasty's little brother JJ, so he just opened the door without asking who it was.

Tayla was standing in front of the door with two hands full of Macy's shopping bags.
"Hey son-in-law!" Tayla greeted with a wide smile as she stepped inside the house.

"Wait until y'all see the outfits I bought my grandbaby!"

Tayla noticed the frown on Dynasty's face.
"What's wrong with you?"
"Nothing", Dynasty replied.

Real smirked as he closed the door knowing that Dynasty was irked with her mother for interrupting the marvelous head she was about to get.

"Move ya fat stank feet so I can sit down!" Tayla joked.
"My feet don't stink!"

Dynasty moved her feet and Tayla giggled as she sat down on the blue leather couch pulling out each item one by one.

"Oh my gosh mom! That outfit is so nice!"

Tayla was holding up a white and pink flower dress with the hat and sandals to match. Real sat across from them and watched as Dynasty and Tayla went through the adorable baby clothes Tayla bought for her granddaughter.

Forty-five minutes later, Real sat on the couch watching TV bored out of his mind while the ladies cooked in the cozy little kitchen frying boneless fish, dirty rice, and sweet corn. Just then another knock came at the door.
"Who is it?" Real asked.
"It's JJ!"

Real unlocked the door.

"What it is bruh?" JJ greeted as he stepped inside the house.
"I'm cooling", Real responded dryly as he went back over to the couch and sat down.
"Damn bruh, you look bored as hell!"

JJ closed the front door and stepped in. He heard his mother and sister in the kitchen laughing and talking loud.
"Let me go give this money to my momma real quick and then I'm going to show you around the town."

After JJ gave his mother the money for the electric bill, he and Real walked out of the house and got inside his green mini van. A feeling of relief came over Real, because he was finally able to get out of the house and get some much needed fresh air. He was tired of being cooped up in the house with Dynasty.

"Im'a go bust this trap then we gon' tour the town" JJ told him as he pulled off.

Oh this nigga down here hustling! I wonder what he moving, Real thought nodding his head and putting his seat belt on.

Once JJ served his sell, not only did he give Real a tour through the entire town, but he also told him everything there was to know about the town. This information was vital to Real since he and Dynasty were moving down there permanently. JJ schooled him on everybody from the small hustlers, the heavy hitting crews that were really touching paper, the stickup kids, the certified killers, the scandalous hood rats who would try to get with you if they thought you were getting money, to the police and how they operated. Real soaked up all the information JJ gave him like a sponge as a masterful plan began to form in the back of his mind.

A few hours had passed and JJ was driving on the freeway back to Real's house.

"So how much you pay for a gram?" Real asked.

"I pay $50 but my peoples charge everybody else $60", JJ replied without taking his eyes off the road.

"Damn! You pay $50 dollars a gram? That's crazy!" Real replied in disbelief.

I can come down here and make millions in no time! Real thought. He began to calculate the profit he would make if he sold it a little cheaper.

"Do you have anything on you right now?"

"Yeah, I got some on me", JJ said digging in his pocket pulling out a bag with a few grams of coke.

JJ handed the bag to Real. Real opened the plastic bag and examined the powder substance.

"Just like I thought, this shit been stepped on like four times!" Real said.

He twisted the bag and handed it back.

"How long does it take you to move a key?"

"A whole key?" JJ repeated as he took his wide eyes off the road and glanced at Real.

JJ had never possessed that much coke at one time a day in his life.

"Damn! Well let me see, probably like five days."

That ain't too bad, Real thought.

"Do you have a team of loyal niggas?"

It took JJ several seconds to respond, thinking seriously of all the dudes he dealt with on the get money tip.

"Yeah, something like that. There's a few dudes I grind and get it with", JJ told him.

Real nodded his head as he stared at him intensely.

"So you sure you can move a key in that amount of time?"

Real had to double check. The last thing he wanted to do was bring some work down here and sit on it.

"Yeah I'm sure", JJ said confidently.

"Well we about to get rich then", Real stated charismatically.

Real knew one key in 5 days was going to turn into 5 keys being moved in one day once things got jumping.

JJ finally pulled in front of Real's house.

"Aight my nigga. I'm gon' have something for you in a few weeks", Real announced as the two slapped hands.

"Aight bruh, I'll be waiting", JJ responded.

After JJ pulled off and was far enough down the street Real walked to his car keeping one eye on the front door. He hoped Dynasty and Tayla didn't hear him getting out of the van causing them to peek out the window. Real hurriedly started the ignition and pulled off looking at the house through his rear view.

Real was on his way back to Trenton. He didn't want to go about it this way but felt he had no choice. Real realized while he and

Dynasty were arguing, that he would not be able to maneuver as long as she was around, so he decided to use her idea of moving out the 'hood to his advantage. His intentions were to move down south to start a new life, but not until he handled everything related to Kaze's tragic situation.

With Dynasty out of the way, Real could handle everything that needed to be taken care of without any distractions. Real left $500,000 cash for Dynasty so she and his daughter could live comfortably if anything were to happen to him.

During the ride back to Trenton, Snake Eyes finally called with all the information that was needed. Real learned not to talk over the phone so he told Snake Eyes to meet him at the hospital where they could talk in person.

Dynasty was sitting on the couch watching TV when her mother walked out of the kitchen eating a bowl of chocolate ice cream.

"Girl, call JJ and make sure they're alright. It's been hours since they've been gone", Tayla said concerned.

"I know, right?"

Dynasty picked up the cordless phone from off the marble table.

"Hello?" JJ answered sounding as if he just woke up.

"JJ where are y'all at? Y'all been gone all day."

"I'm in the house with my lady."

"So where the hell Real at?"

"I dropped him off in front of y'all house like six hours ago."

"Six hours ago!" Dynasty yelled dropping the phone.

Dynasty got up and ran out of the house.

"Chile what happened? Don't be running like that with my grandbaby in your stomach!" Tayla shouted trotting behind her.

Dynasty made it to the porch steps and immediately began crying hysterically, she knew exactly where Real went.

"What's wrong baby?" Tayla asked worried, comforting her daughter.
"He left!"

Tayla looked and noticed that Real's car was gone.
"Where did he go?"
"Back to raggedy ass Trenton!" Dynasty cried.

Dynasty was so angry with Real for deceiving her, but she was madder at herself for believing him. *How could I be so stupid? I should've known Real wouldn't just up and leave after what happened to Kaze*, Dynasty said to herself.

"Calm down baby, he'll be back", Tayla said trying to comfort Dynasty by placing her hand on the middle of her back.

Dynasty turned around and stormed back into the house. She picked up the phone furiously dialing Real's cell number but it went straight to voicemail.

"I hate you!" She screamed angrily as she threw the cordless phone against the wall with all her might.

Dynasty flopped down on the couch and buried her face into her hands crying.

****

Real finally reached Trenton. As soon as he stepped inside Kaze's hospital room Carla rushed at him crying uncontrollably.

"Real I can't take this anymore."

Carla wrapped her arms around Real, holding him tightly. Real noticed Snake Eyes in all black standing near the window sadly shaking his head from side to side.

"I can't stand to see my baby suffering like this. He's dead Real, Kaze's dead."

Carla released Real from her embrace. Real looked into Carla's face and noticed the heavy bags under her puffy red eyes. It looked like she'd been crying and been without sleep ever since the day Kaze was shot. Real could only imagine how she felt since Kaze was her only child.

"Listen, I know I said it's up to you to pull the plug, and I'm going to stick to my word. But look at my son Real, he's suffering."

Real looked down at Kaze and his heart began to ache as the camera in the back of his mind flashed back to all the good and bad times they shared together. The time Kaze let him wear his clothes so he wouldn't have to wear PAY-LESS to school. The time they both started hustling together. The time they lost their virginity together. The time Kaze stood up and took the murder charge on the chin to set Real free. Kaze was always by Real's side which picked at his soul. The one time Kaze needed him the most, he wasn't there.

"Real do you hear me?" Carla asked.

Real snapped out of his trip down memory lane.

"Huh?"

"Kaze's gone baby. The ventilator is breathing for him, but he's gone. You're just wasting your money."

Real sighed as he sat down in the chair next to his best friend with his head hung low. *Damn man, I just can't pull the plug on Kaze like that*, he said to himself somberly as the logic behind Carla's words began to sink in.

Snake Eyes walked up from behind and placed his hand on Real's shoulder.

"She's right my nigga, he's gone. All we can do now is handle our handle", he said sadly.

Snake Eyes dug in his pocket, and pulled out a white envelope.

"Everything we need to know is inside here."

Real grabbed the envelope out of Snake Eyes hand and stood up. He again turned to face Carla.

"Let me holla at him in the hallway. I'll be right back."

Carla nodded.

When Snakes Eyes and Real exited the room, Real read every page and looked at the pictures in the envelope. All the information was there. Fletcho was the one who put the hit out on Kaze and everyone he loved including Real. Snake Eyes told Real that Fletcho wanted Kaze murdered because the young kid Ricky was his cousin. Snake Eyes told Real that he could get plenty of money after killing Fletcho. He was getting major paper and had people on different blocks hustling for him. One of Fletcho's blocks was around the corner from Snake Eyes's block, so it was nothing for him to get the drop on him.

"So when you want to move out on this bitch ass nigga?" Snake Eyes asked looking into Real's blood shot eyes.
"Tonight!" Real stated firmly.

Real looked down at his Rolex for the time.

"It's 12:30, I want you to meet me on Chase st. at 3 o'clock", Real ordered.

"Let's go now! I know that nigga in the house!" Snake Eyes suggested.

"Nah, I got to go handle something else first", Real said with devilish grin. "I'm about to go back inside and holla at Kaze's mom. I'll see you at 3 o'clock."

They slapped hands.

"Aight bruh", Snake Eyes said before walking down the bright hospital corridor.

Real stepped back in.

"This is a hard decision for me to make. I need a few hours to clear my head. It's 12:30 now, I'll be back around 3:30-4:00 with my mind made up."

"I understand Real. It is a tough decision go clear your mind and I'll be here when you get back", Carla said.

Real hugged Carla and took another look at Kaze and all of the tubes and wires before leaving.

Once Real handled what was necessary he went straight to Chase Street. He sat on the curb between two big trucks holding a black bag with duct tape, a glass cutter, and rope inside. *Man where the fuck this nigga at,* Real said to himself.

Within minutes he heard footsteps coming towards him. He poked his head out to see that it was Snake Eyes. When Real stood up holding the gym bag, he startled Snake Eyes who reached for the pistol in his waist line.

"Oh shit! I ain't even see you right there", Snake Eyes said stopping in his tracks.
"Where you park at?" Real asked.
"Around the corner", Snake Eyes said eyeing the black bag. "What's in the bag?"
"Duct tape, rope, and a glass cutter."

Snake Eyes looked puzzled. He thought they were just going to run inside the house, shoot Fletcho and rob the place.
"What's all that for?"
"So this nigga won't try no slick shit while we take him to one of my spots."

What the fuck this nigga keep asking me all these questions for, Real thought.

They walked across the street and crept along the side of Fletcho's house. Once they got to the last window near the backyard, Real took his glass cutter out of his bag and carefully cut the glass from out the bottom part of the window. Snake Eyes followed Real inside.

The lights were off which made the house pitch black. They both pulled out their guns and navigated through the kitchen straining their eyes to see in the darkness. When they made it to the living room they began to hear loud moans coming from upstairs.

"We just in time. His bitch ass upstairs inside some pussy!" Snake Eyes whispered.

They quietly snuck upstairs with their guns drawn and crept towards the room where the grunts were coming from.
"Aww daddy! Fuck me good! Ooh yes!" The female voice moaned.

The door was cracked open. When Real peeked inside he shook his head and smirked at the sight before him. Fletcho was in the bed completely naked and knocked out sleep with a big ass bottle of lotion on the dresser while a porno played on the flatscreen.

"Oh that dick so good!" The girl in the movie moaned.
"Man look at this shit!" Real whispered looking back at Snake Eyes.

Snake Eyes entered the room and chuckled at the hilarious scene.

As they approached the bed Fletcho began sluggishly shifting around. He opened his eyes to see two masked men standing over him.
"Oh shit!" He yelled in a high tone.

Fletcho's eyes showed fear.
"What y'all want? I'll give y'all whatever y'all want!" Fletcho pleaded scared for his life.
"Nigga we want you!" Real growled.

Real smacked Fletcho in the head with the butt of the gun knocking him out.

"Hurry up and tie this nigga up!" Real ordered, grabbing the duct take and rope.

Real and Snake Eyes quickly hog-tied Fletcho and carried him out the back door. They threw him in the black van Real parked in the alley in back of the house.

15 minutes later, Real pulled behind an abandoned building and put the van in park. Snake Eyes slid the van door open as Real hopped out to assist him. They carried Fletcho, who was now woke, inside the abandoned building and threw him on a piss-filled dirty mattress that was laying in the middle of the living room floor. The unstable building was old and dusty with holes in the walls and floor.

"Umm...Umm." Fletcho struggled to talk through the duct tape covering his mouth.

Real looked at Snake Eyes.

"It seem like he got a whole lot to say!"

"I know right?" Snake Eyes agreed, forcefully snatching the tape from his mouth causing the skin on his lips to peel off.

"Agghh!" Fletcho yelled painfully as his lips began to bleed.

"Shut the fuck up before I blow ya brains out ya head!" Real threatened, placing the barrel of his black 9mm on Fletcho's forehead.

Fletcho managed to keep quiet for a few seconds, but started begging desperately in a low tone.

"Please don't kill me. I got money, that's what this is about right?"

"I don't need ya money nigga!" Real frowned.

"Don't play stupid! You know what this is about!" Snake Eyes added pistol-whipping Fletcho.

"Agghh!" Fletcho screamed as Snake Eyes continued to beat him across the head with his .357 Magnum.

Snake Eyes split Fletcho's head to the white meat, and thick globs of blood began pouring on to the filthy mattress.

Real watched for a few seconds.
"Hold on. I'll be right back."

Real ran up the raggedy stairs. He opened the door to the first room on the left and went inside. When Real stepped out the room, he held a thick chain in his hand with a slim brown skin woman shackled to it. She was completely nude with duct tape covering her mouth and a thick black scarf tied around the top part of her face, concealing her identity.

Real led her down the stairs and threw her on the edge of the dirty, bloody mattress. Snake Eyes was still pistol whipping Fletcho.

"Please stop!" Fletcho begged.

Fletcho's face was black and purple and he was bleeding profusely.

"Untie him", Real ordered.

Breathing heavily Snake Eyes stopped and noticed the naked slim lady sitting on the edge of the mattress. *Who the fuck is that?,* he thought to himself puzzled staring at the shackled lady. He was so into torturing Fletcho he didn't notice when Real came down the stairs with her. Snake Eyes handed Real the bloody Magnum and then untied Fletcho.

"You try any funny shit and you a dead man!" Real warned firmly as he pointed the gun in Fletcho's bloody face, holding his 9mm in his other hand.

"Okay! Okay! Please, just don't kill me!" Fletcho cried shaking uncontrollably glancing at the lady sitting on the edge of the mattress.

"You say you want to live right?" Real asked.
"Yeah, man, Yeah! I'll do whatever just please don't kill me!"
"Aight bend her over and fuck her in the ass", Real commanded as he waved his gun towards the naked lady.

"Aww man this some bullshit! What you about to make me fuck somebody with AIDS?" Fletcho cried looking at the slim naked lady.

"Do it or die!", Real said through clenched teeth as he cocked back the hammer ready to blow Fletchos brains all over the mattress.

What the fuck type of shit this nigga on, Snake Eyes thought as he watched Fletcho slide his manhood raw dog inside her anally. He began to slowly stroke her.

"Fuck her harder!" Real barked in Fletcho's ear.

Fletcho began to thrust harder and harder grabbing her by the waist, causing the lady to squirm and try to get away. She bled and defecated on Fletcho's manhood. The excruciating pain from him forcefully thrusting his 10 inch manhood in and out of her caused her to scream from the top of her lungs, but the duck tape over her mouth muffled the sound.

The terrible smell of blood, shit, and fear spread throughout the living room. Fletcho was still pounding the woman's back out relentlessly when Real snatched the black scarf off from around her face.

Real let out a loud wicked laugh. Fletcho's eyes grew wide, he immediately stopped and vomited at the sight!

"No! Mom!" He shouted in disbelief as his mother turned her ravaged body to look back at him.

Her face was full of tears. Fletcho turned his mother around and sat on the edge of the bed close beside her. He wrapped his arms around her and started crying like a baby.
"Aww mom, I'm sorry. I'm so sorry", he cried.

Not only was Fletcho devastated, he was disgusted with himself.

Snake Eyes was flabbergasted as he watched everything play out. Real took all of the bullets out of the .357 and handed it to Fletcho. *What the fuck this crazy ass nigga doing now,* Snake Eyes said to himself not knowing what to expect next. Real pointed his black 9mm at Fletcho's head.

"Aight, this how this shit gon' go, you either gon' murder yourself, or I'm going to murder you and your mom."

Fletcho swallowed hard as he looked into his mother's teary eyes.

"I'm sorry mom. I don't know what's going on! Please forgive me!" he cried.

There was no way to know if Real was lying or not but Fletcho was inclined to take that chance to save his mother's life. Without pleading for his life, he stuck the barrel of the gun in his mouth and pulled the trigger. BOOM! Fletcho's brains splattered all over his mother's face as his lifeless body fell backwards onto the filthy mattress. Fletcho wouldn't have been able to live with himself after doing what he did to his mother.

Eventually he would have committed suicide anyway.

Real removed the duct tape from Fletcho's mother's trembling lips and unshackled one of her hands before he and Snake Eyes rushed out of the abandoned building, hopped back into the van, and sped off.

****

Carla was knocked out sleep next to Kaze's bedside holding his hand when Real and Snake Eyes walked through the hospital room door waking her.

"Sorry it took so long, we had to handle some serious business", Real said as he gently placed his hand on her shoulder.

Snake Eyes stood a few feet away from the sink.

"It's okay baby", Carla said, letting out a light yawn. "So, what did you decide to do?" She asked.

Real looked down at Kaze and sighed deeply as he shook his head. He had already decided on what he was going to do before he left the hospital earlier. He just wanted to make sure the man responsible for Kaze getting shot was dead and gone before the plug was pulled.

Real thought doing what he did would make him feel better, but it didn't. He was still sick to his stomach. Real fought back the tears that burned his eyes as he looked at Carla.
"Tell 'em to pull it", he said sadly.

A sad smile rose on Carla's face. Silent tears fell from her eyes. She was sad that her only son's life was officially ending, but was glad he no longer had to suffer.

"Alright, I'll go tell the doctors", she said leaving out the room.

Real, Carla, and Snake Eyes stood at Kaze's bedside. Carla was sniffling and wiping the tears from her face as she watched the doctor and nurses enter the room. Real leaned down and whispered in Kaze's ear.

"I'm sorry bruh...I slipped up. Please forgive me."

The doctor turned off the ventilator. BEEEEP! The loud sound echoed throughout the hospital room. Tears began falling down Real's cheeks as he looked back and stared at Kaze's lifeless body. Snake Eyes saw that Kaze's mother was about to break down so he hugged her, keeping her from falling. "Everything's going to be alright. He's in a better place", he offered trying to comfort her. Carla cried her heart out on his chest, as Snake Eyes gently rubbed her back.

CHAPTER 10

During the several days before Kaze's funeral, it rained bullets and blood throughout the entire city. Not only did Real's team and Snake Eyes' squad form an alliance that wiped out Fletcho's crew, but they also terminated all the other competition throughout the city in the process. Snake Eyes put his workers on all the deserted blocks with coke to move while recruiting new soldiers daily, building a stronger army.

Real, on the other hand, didn't rock with new niggas. He kept his team the same. Plus he figured since Snakes Eyes had workers and soldiers everywhere and Real supplied him, there was no need to switch up. Together they conquered the entire city.

At Kaze's funeral, all that was heard was the sad and slow hymns playing throughout the church speakers . The pastor stood before everyone in attendance reading Psalms 59:62. Kamikaze lay in his silver-plated casket looking as if he were sleeping peacefully. He wore an all white Prada suit with a royal blue tie and had his cornrows neatly braided. Real wore the exact same suit but in black. He sat in the front pew along with Carla, Qadeesha and a few of Kaze's other relatives.

Dose and the rest of Real's entourage sat in the pews behind Real and Kaze's family, while Snake Eyes and his squad took up the first five pews on the opposite side of the church. Even though most of Snake Eyes soldiers never met Kaze, they still came to show respect off the strength of Real.

The church was jam packed! It looked as if the entire city of Trenton had come to say their final farewell to the young stand-up gangster. *Damn my nigga really dead*, Real thought again and again while watching the long line of people waiting their turn to get a close and final look at Kaze.

A few hustlers and gangsters dropped wads of cash and jewelry in the casket while others said their goodbyes and kept it moving. Carla couldn't believe how many people came.

"Kaze probably ain't know half of these people", she said to Qadeesha who sat beside her.

"I know", Qadeesha agreed.

The two were mourning but no tears escaped their eyes. They had been crying for days.

Snake Eyes and Real's eyes both grew wide when they saw a beautiful female approach Kaze's casket. She kissed Kaze on the forehead and whispered something in his ear. *Damn who the fuck is that. She bad as hell,* Snake Eyes said to himself in amazement as he watched the exotic creature.

The whole time Real was thinking, *Damn, when the fuck she get down here!* He watched Dynasty turn away from Kaze's casket and begin to walk in his direction. She had her hair cut like Rihanna's which brought out her exotic facial features. The sleeveless white and burgundy designer dress she wore revealed the extra pounds she put on in all the right places. The only way you could tell she was pregnant is if you got close up on her.

Without looking at Real, Dynasty walked past him as if he wasn't even there. *Lying ass nigga,* she thought.

"Damn girl, what took you so long", Qadeesha asked hugging Dynasty.
"I missed the first train and had to wait 2 hours for the next one", Dynasty explained sitting next to her cousin.

Dynasty saw the sadness in Qadeesha's eyes and immediately felt bad for not being around to support her cousin.
"Are you alright big cousin?"
"I'm doing better."

Qadeesha felt cheated. She had waited patiently and faithfully for 4 years for Kaze to come home. She hadn't had a chance to spend a full day with him. He was murdered in cold blood right in front of her own eyes.

While Real was trying to figure out what he was going to say to Dynasty, Snake Eyes' lustful eyes were locked on her. His right hand man Low Down was sitting beside him and noticed he was staring at the exotic looking red headed redbone.

"Damn, who that?" He asked Snake Eyes.

"I don't know but whoever it is she about to be mine."

Snake Eyes could only assume that Dynasty was family since she was sitting in the front pew.

Dynasty felt her cell phone vibrating in her purse.

"I'll be right back", she said to Qadeesha as she got up.

Real quickly got up and followed her. Snake Eyes did the same exact thing.

"Hello?" Dynasty answered.

"Hey baby, are you alright", Tayla asked.

"Yeah mom, I'm good. I made it here safe and sound."

Dynasty saw Real coming towards her from the corner of her eye and started speed walking past the several people that stood in front of the church.

"Mom I'm at the funeral. I'll call you back once it's over."

Real walked close behind her.
"Dynasty!" He shouted.

Dynasty ignored him and kept it moving. *I don't know what the hell he calling me for,* she said to herself with an attitude as she continued speed walking.

"Dynasty!" Real shouted again jogging behind her.

Dynasty glanced behind and saw Real running up on her.
"If this nigga just don't leave me the hell alone", she murmured.

Real grabbed her by the wrist stopping her in her tracks.
"Why you acting all crazy?" He asked.
"Let me the fuck go!"

Dynasty tried to break loose from Real's grasp but couldn't.

"Chill out!" He demanded trying to calm her down.

Dynasty knew they were making a scene, but still didn't give a damn.

"I don't want to hear that chill out shit! You left me and the baby down their all alone. Fuck you!"
"I love you and my daughter. I left y'all down there so y'all could be safe! If I wouldn't have done it that way, you would've been on my every move, and that would've distracted me while I was handling my handle."

Snake Eyes was standing a few feet away from the church doors with his arms folded across his chest watching the two go back and forth. *Damn man, this must be this nigga wifey or some shit*, he said to himself enviously. Snake Eyes couldn't actually hear what they were saying, but he could tell by their body language and gestures that they were having a serious argument.

Real noticed that Dynasty was lost for words, and knew that his logic was sinking in.
"Baby I'm sorry", he stated smoothly looking deep into Dynasty's green eyes.

Real released her wrist and gently grabbed her by the hand, intertwining his fingers with hers and gave her a passionate kiss.

"Everything's done and over with now. Let's just forget it ever happened and move on", Real said trying his best to make up.

Dynasty poked out her full pink lips. She immediately forgave him, but still had a little attitude.
"Ya black ass still ain't have to lie to me."

Real led her back towards the church. Snake Eyes was still waiting outside.
"You aight my nigga?"He asked Real.
"Yeah, I'm good", Real responded.

Snake Eyes glanced down and immediately noticed the bubble in Dynasty's stomach. *Damn, this nigga her baby daddy!* He thought.

"It look like somebody got a baby on the way", he joked with Real.

"Oh yeah, um…this my baby mom Dynasty, Dynasty this my nigga Snake Eyes."

"What's good Dynasty", Snake Eyes greeted trying to conceal his admiration.

Get the fuck out of here! If this was really ya nigga I would've been met his ass! Dynasty said to herself.

Barely even looking at Snake Eyes, Dynasty waved as she released her other hand from Real's grasp and walked back into the church. Real shook his head smirking.

"Don't mind her my nigga, that's just how she is. She be on her shit 24-7 since she been pregnant", he told Snake Eyes as they both walked back in to the church.

Later on that night, Real and All Things were seated at a table across from one another in the basement of Real's beauty shop having a personal meeting.

"I'm aware of everything that's been going on the last few weeks. That's why I called to tell you that it was urgent that we meet up", All Things stated calmly.

All Things could tell by the stress lines on Real's forehead and the sadness in his eyes that he was taking his best friend's death very hard.

Real wasn't surprised when he heard what All Things had to say. He just nodded his head and waited to hear whatever it was he was going to say next.

"First off, I'm sorry to hear about Kaze, but the heinous acts that were committed during the two weeks after his death got the streets terrified which can prove to be very profitable for the both of us."

Real raised an eyebrow. He knew that more money was about to start rolling in due to the takeover his team and Snake Eyes' squad made happen, but he didn't realize the full potential of the opportunity. All Things noticed the confused look on Real's face.

"Any and every nigga that's getting money in them streets gon' listen to whatever you tell them to do. Which means you can sprinkle coke in every hood and raise the prices to whatever you want."

Real leaned back in his seat and thought about what All Things said for a few seconds and it all made sense. He calculated all the extra money he would make once he raised the price.

"Damn you know what, you're right."

"Yeah, I know I'm right", All Things shot back grinning.

The more blocks Real supplied and the higher he raised the prices, meant the more money he would make, which resulted in him spending more money with All Things. All Things wasn't just crafty, ruthless and cunning when it came to maneuvering the streets, he was also what you called a smart and savvy business man.

"Listen, I'm going to have my best man stand by your side and be the yes behind your head and trigger finger if need be. Just in case any outsiders or any of your own men try to get you out of the picture."

None of my niggas would ever do no shit like that! Real thought frowning.
"No disrespect All Things, but I don't need no help from nobody. Me and my niggas got everything under control."

Although Real looked at All Things as a father-figure and knew that his word was gold, he just couldn't see himself allowing someone new into his immediate circle.

All Things slammed his fist against the table. "What I'm saying to you is not a request. It's something that must happen."

Real blinked his eyes in shock. He had never seen All Things loose his composure.

"Ya own mother will stab you in the back over an opportunity like this. So just imagine what the niggas close to you will do."

All Things stopped talking and just stared at Real. He could tell that his words affected him.

"That's where my man Wild Sal comes in to play. He's going to prevent any of that from happening, that's what he's trained to do. Shit if it wasn't for him, I would've been dead a long time ago."

All Things mind briefly wandered back to the several times Wild Sal saved his life.
"Trust me when I tell you he's the best of the best."

Real let out a deep breath and sat back in the seat. Real knew that All Things would never put him in harm's way, and he never told him anything inaccurate since he knew him. Because of that he agreed even though he really didn't want to.

"Aight man. When I'm gon' meet the nigga."
"Hold on I'm about to get him. He's outside on guard right now."

All Things got up from his seat and walked up the basement steps. He returned with Wild walking behind him.
"Wild Sal, this is Real, Real, Wild Sal."

Real stood and slapped hands with Wild Sal.
"What's good?"
"You and all the great things I've heard about you", Wild Sal responded.

His name fit his wild looking appearance. He was a short cocky older guy with wild looking long dreads and a thick long beard. He didn't talk much and loved and lived for war. Wild Sal hunted and crept up on his prey like a lion in the jungle, and got a thrill out of seeing the shocking looks on their faces right before he took their lives away.

Everyone sat down at the round table and began discussing how they were going to go about handling things.

A few months later, Real was about to get ready to go with all his soldiers on the tour buses they rented for their trip down Miami to celebrate his birthday. It was 5 o'clock in the morning. Real lay in his king size bed with nothing on but his red and white silk boxers. Dynasty lay beside him in her silk bra and panties resting on his chiseled chest. From the size of her belly you would've thought she was having twins. The baby was due in two weeks and Dynasty who was extremely anxious couldn't wait for the day her little princess came into the world.

Real's eyes popped open when he heard his cell phone vibrating on the nightstand. He reached to grab his phone. Dynasty's eyes slowly opened.

"Yo?" Real answered.

"Damn bro what's up. I'm out front waiting right now. You know we gotta collect that paper and dish out the work a lot earlier so we can make it to Miami on time", Snake Eyes reminded.

"Yeah you right. I'm on my way down right now."

Real rushed out of bed. Dynasty rubbed her eyes as she sat up in the bed and watched Real get dressed. She knew about the trip and was mad because Real wouldn't allow her to go since she was pregnant. She was impatient and upset about a few other things also.

"So you about to go on ya little birthday trip and have a whole bunch of fun, huh?"
"Yeah, I guess you can say that. I'ma take some pictures for you."

Real began putting on his jewelry.

This nigga gotta be fucking kidding me, Dynastly thought to herself, chuckling sarcastically. "Whatever happened to the Real I used to know...The Real that used to be a man of his word?" Dynasty asked still trying to keep her cool.

Real couldn't wait until the day Dynasty had the baby. He was excited to be able to hold his baby girl, but he also couldn't wait for Dynasty to stop having all her damn mood swings.

"Here we go with this shit again. What is it now Dynasty?"

Real walked to the edge of the bed and sat beside her.

"You said as soon as you put everything in order we were going back down south to start a new and better life. That was months ago, and I know everything is in order by now."

Real looked down at the floor. His intent was to go back down south, but it seemed like every time he was about to make the move, something always happened that required him to stay in the city.

"Not only that, it's like there is something missing about you."

Dynasty was right. Ever since he lost Kaze, it was like he lost a big piece of himself. She couldn't really pinpoint what it was, but he wasn't the same *on top of his game Real*.

"Baby, I'm still a man of my word. Ain't nothing change about me. I just got caught up in the moment that's all. We're going to move back down south after you have the baby."

"You ain't just gon' up and leave us down there like you did last time are you?"

"Nah babes, I ain't ever doing no shit like that again, I promise. If I got to make a quick run back to the city, you'll be the first to know about it, aight."

Real placed his finger beneath Dynasty's chin, leaned forward, and softly kissed her on the lips.

BEEP! BEEP! BEEP! Snake Eyes was out front blowing the horn.

"Aight baby, I got to go. I'll see you when I get back, I love you", Real told Dynasty before rushing out of the house.

Real jumped in Snake Eyes' blue Jaguar coup and the two rode around the whole entire city for almost an hour, collecting lump sums of cash and dropping off large amounts of coke and dope. Snake Eyes introduced Real to the dope game 3 months ago, and Real appreciated him dearly for it. Real turned a profit from selling coke in one month, but he profited damn near double from selling herion in a week. The flip was crazy! As the famous saying goes: *It ain't no money like dope money*.

Snake Eyes tried to speed through a yellow light but it turned red.
"Damn!" He exclaimed as he slammed his foot on the break, scanning for police.

When it was pickup and drop off time, Snake Eyes tried to move as swiftly and precise as possible, especially when he had three duffle bags filled with cash in the trunk. Real was leaned back in the passenger seat. He pulled out a misplaced baggie of heroin from his True Religion pant's pocket. The stamp on it read *Super Lean*. It was the best dope in the city.

Damn...this is what took my mom away from me when I was younger. This what she chose over me,

Real thought while staring down at the package of dope. Deep in his heart he felt like dope owed him something, and although the effect the drug had on his mother and childhood was extremely costly, he silently made a vow that he would make more money than any other hustler did off the product.

Snake Eyes turned to see Real staring down at the package of dope in his hand.
"Man if you don't hurry up and throw that shit out the window! If them people pull us over, and find that shit we won't be able to getting a dollar back!" He said paranoid.

"Yeah you right", Real agreed tossing the dope package out as hard as he could.

Real knew exactly what Snake Eyes was talking about because the police caught Dose with one bag of heroin, and took $40 grand from him. Real had his big sister try to get the money back by claiming that it was hers because she had a few legitimate businesses, but the officials considered the lump sum drug money, and said she wouldn't be able to get it back.

As Snake Eyes pulled off from the light he asked, "Which spot you want to drop the bread off at?"

Snake Eyes and Real had a stash house on every side of the city.

"Take it to the spot across the street from my mom's house", Real replied.

Snake Eyes knew where Real's mother lived but he had never met her.

"Aight", Snake Eyes said turning down a side street.

Unbeknownst to Snake Eyes, he was being followed ever since he pulled off from Real's house, and it wasn't by the police or the stick up kids. It was Wild Sal, Real's extra set of eyes when he was unable to see and his extra pair of hands when he was unable to reach out and touch. For Wild Sal, this procedure was as normal as waking up and brushing his teeth in the morning. He would usually follow Real around for a few hours, then call and ask where he was, as if he didn't already know. After Real gave him his location the two would always meet up.

Snake Eyes parked the car in front of the stash house. Real rushed out of the car grabbing the duffle bags of cash. Snake Eyes was beside him surveying the area with his hand on his strap, quickly leading Real into the stash house. Once they stashed the money in the bathroom ceiling they left out.

"Aight business is over with. Now it's time to take it down to Miami and enjoy your birthday", Snake Eyes said while him and Real walked to his Jaguar.

Suddenly, a female voice yelled.
"Real!"

Real recognized the voice and turned to see his mother standing in the door way of her house. She wore a pink robe and a pink and white scarf around her head. *She must've been looking out the window,* Real thought.

"Come over here bruh, let me introduce you to my mom", Real said.

Real jogged up the steps and gave his mother a hug.

"What's going on mom", he greeted with Snake Eyes right behind him.

"Happy birthday baby."

"Mom I want you to meet my friend Snake Eyes."

Real stepped aside to introduce him. As soon as Snake Eyes stepped on the porch his eyes grew wide. *Oh shit! That's his mom,* Snake Eyes said to himself in disbelief.

Nyla was thinking almost the same exact thing. *Oh my gosh, what is Snake Eyes doing with my son,* she thought trying to keep her nervousness concealed.

Nyla had been one of Snake Eyes' most loyal customers for the last two and a half years! Sometimes she would even exchange sex for drugs when she couldn't support her addiction.

"Pleased to meet you miss. My real name is Shawn", Snake Eyes introduced himself playing it off.

Nyla went right along with him as a fake smile crept across her face.
"My name Nyla, Shawn."

Nyla hoped to God that Snake Eyes wouldn't give it away that she was still using heroin. Real picked up on the weird vibe, but didn't think too much into it.

"So you was just going to come through and not stop by ya mom house to make sure she was doing aight, huh?" Nyla asked.
"Nah mom, you know it ain't like that. I'm just in a rush. We about to go to Miami to celebrate my birthday", Real explained.
"Oooh Miami sounds like fun. So where's my two li'l mamas?"
"In the house", Real replied.

"I know she probably in that house bored out of her mind. Probably eating up everything in the refrigerator with her fat self. Matter fact, I'm about to call her."

"Yeah mom, you do that. We about to go hop on this bus. I love you."

"Alright son, I love you and y'all be safe."

Real and Snake Eyes left the porch steps, climbed inside the car, and pulled off.

It would be one thing to learn that Nyla was up to her old tricks again, but for Real to find out that Snake Eyes was her supplier would be entirely too much. There's no telling how he would've reacted.

CHAPTER 11

During the long ride to Miami, Real's and Snake Eyes' entourage filled every seat on both of their tour buses. Bottles of liquor and blunts of the best chronic money could buy circulated in rotation back and forth. They were gambling, making comical jokes on one another and laughing uncontrollably, and listening to music. They had several camcorders recording every moment.

Real had just got off the phone with the realtor about their Miami rental house. He didn't smoke, but he had drunk a little bit of liquor. The only one that stayed sober was Wild Sal, who was always on point. Even though it was only family around, he kept his eye on Real and made sure he drank out of his own personal Henny bottles.

The tour buses finally arrived in the city of Miami, and the crowd of young hustlers was excited, realizing that the world is way bigger than the slums of Trenton. Their eyes viewed the unique look of the tropical city in amazement. Palm trees stood as tall as the buildings, exotic women seemed to be everywhere you looked, and mostly foreign cars sped up and down the wide streets.

Seeing a Benz was like seeing a hoopty in Trenton. Real noticed how everyone was riding hard and said *fuck that*. He got out of his seat, walked up to the front of the bus, and tapped the driver on the shoulder. The driver glanced up at Real and then focused his eyes back on the road.
"Take us to the biggest car lot in Miami!" Real ordered.

Both tour buses pulled up in front of a huge car lot. Real stood up from his seat to make an announcement.
"We gonna make our presence felt while we down here!"

Real then walked up to the driver and gave him a thousand dollar tip.
"I'm gon' call you in two days", he told him.

The driver looked up at Real and smiled.

"Thanks."

Real stepped off the bus and looked up at the billboard in front of the car lot which read: BIG DEALS-BEST WHEELS. They all bum-rushed the car lot, spreading out looking at all the exotic cars. A variety of top of the line cars such as Bentleys, Porshes, Aston Martins, Maybachs, Farraris, and Benzes lined the lot.

The few onlookers that were there to purchase cars stopped and stared in awe. The staff thought they were under attack when they saw the enormous crowd of young men swarm. Real, Snake Eyes, Dose, and of course Wild Sal stepped inside the spacious office. A beautiful black clerk sat behind a wooden desk typing on a computer.

"Where the hell the dealer at?" Real asked cockily as he swaggered towards the clerk.

Real sat in the chair across from her and kicked his Prada shoes up on the desk. The clerk looked at him in shock then glanced at Snake Eyes, Dose, and Wild Sal, who were standing near the entrance door. Real noticed the look in her eyes and smirked.

"Who are you sir?" She asked.

"The realest mufucka ever born", Real replied.

Snake Eyes and Dose chuckled while Wild Sal just stood there with his arms folded across his chest. The clerk immediately got on the phone and called for a dealer to come up to the front. The dealer immediately appeared. He was a short Italian man with black silky hair combed to the back.

"How may I help you gentlemen", he asked.

The dealer noticed that Real was resting his shoes on the clerk's desk. *Who the fuck does this guy think he is*, he thought.

"We need 40 cars", Real said boldly.

Real's entourage was 30 deep and Snake Eyes's was 50 deep. The dealer's eyes grew wide.

"You want 40 cars? Who the hell are you? Oprah's son?!"

Real and everyone else in the room couldn't help but laugh.

"Nah, boss man. I'm Nyla's son, and I ain't come to stay. I came to play."

Real saw the confused look on the dealer's face, and knew that he didn't comprehend what he just said.

"I ain't come to buy, I came to rent", he stated smoothly.

"For how long?" the dealer asked.

"Two days."

"Well just to let you know, the lowest priced car on the lot will cost you seven hundred a day to rent."

"That shit ain't 'bout nothing boss man."

Real pulled a wad of cash out of his pocket.

"This $30 grand right here", Real said slamming his money on the desk.

Real looked back at Snake Eyes and Dose. The two both looked at one another sharing the same thought. Real frowned, knowing exactly what they were thinking.

"What the fuck taking y'all so long to go in y'all pocket? All that money y'all be tricking on them hoes, but y'all don't want to spend no money for ya squad to stunt?" Real said shaking his head in disgust.

"Aight man damn! That's 15 racks" Snake Eyes said pulling a wad of cash out of his pocket slamming it down on the desk.

Dose decided to follow suit.

"I got 15 racks too!"

"Now let's go pick out our cars so we can tear this fucking city up", Real said charismatically.

Later on that night, it looked like the biggest car show in the world was taking place as the all white Phantom cruised through the streets of Miami, followed by 40 of the most exotic cars you could possibly think of. Miami was used to expensive cars and big ballers stunting, but not to this degree.

Real sat in the passenger seat of the Phantom. POP! He popped the cork on a bottle of champagne causing suds to spill on the floor.

Snake Eyes and Dose sat in the back guzzling two personal bottles of champagne. Wild Sal, the designated driver, remained completely quiet paying close attention to their surroundings. Real lifted the bottle of champagne in the air.

"I'd like to make a toast to every true to life breadwinner out there in them streets on top of they game!"

Snake Eyes and Dose lifted their bottles in the air and tapped them against Real's bottle, everyone began drinking. They cruised through the city for another hour before pulling in to the parking lot of an enormous club. The cars pulled in back to back, swarming the valet. All eyes were on them, as everyone climbed out of their cars and walked to the front entrance with Real leading the pack. All that was heard were the whispers coming from the long entrance line. The people waiting to get in the club watched in awe as Real and his entourage made their way to the front of the line.

A big, black, bald-headed bouncer stood there. "Listen big dog, this for me and my squad", Real told him.

Real dug in his pocket pulled out a wad of cash and handed it to the bouncer. The bouncer scanned through the wad of cash and saw that it was all crispy hundred dollar bills and stuffed the money in his pants pocket. "Come on", he said with a deep voice, barely patting them down.

You would've thought the president was in the building the way Real's entourage guarded him. Majority of the females gravitated to them, making their way to VIP.

Everyone was dancing, drinking, and having fun when the song *Ball So Hard* by Kanye and Jay Z came on. Snake Eyes shook up a bottle of champagne and popped the cork before pouring it on a brown skinned Dominican female. She wore a very short colorful flower skirt and was bent over with her hands on the bar stool, trying to keep her balance while making her ass clap.

"Yeah! This how Trenton niggas do it! Real big muhfucka!" Snake Eyes shouted looking at Real, Dose, and Wild Sal who were all seated.

Everyone burst out laughing.
 "Snake Eyes shot the fuck out", Dose said laughing.
"Hell yeah! That nigga don't got it all!" Real agreed.

Suddenly, Real saw a shadow appear on the side of him from the corner of his eye.

"What's good my nigga. I see y'all doing it real big in here. I know y'all got a bottle of champagne for ya boy", the young man said as he reached out his hand.

Real looked down at his hand, then looked up at him. His face looked very familiar. Then it clicked, long dreads, dark skin tattoos all over his face and body. Real frowned his face.
"Man if you don't get your funny looking ass out of my face", Real told him harshly.

Lul, the Straight Cash artist, just stood there with a stupid look on his face. He couldn't believe what he just heard.

"What you can't hear or something?" Real said.
"Pardon yourself, you blocking my view", Wild Sal said to Lul.

The Straight Cash rapper walked away, disappearing into the crowd. Dose looked at Real like he lost his mind.
"Do you know who that was my nigga?"

Real took a gigantic gulp of the bottle of champagne and looked at Dose.
"Yeah I know who that was, nigga do you know who the fuck I am?"

A few hours went by and the club was finally about to close, but little did everyone know the real party was just about to begin. Every female in the club followed Real and Snake Eyes into the parking lot. Real and Snake Eyes could barely walk. They both had two Dominican groupies under each arm, keeping them balanced as they followed behind Dose and Wild Sal.

Dose opened the Phantom doors turning to face the enormous crowd, raising a bottle of champagne in the air.
"After party at the mansion! Females only follow us!"

Dose then climbed inside the Phantom, along with Snake Eyes and Real, Wild Sal and the 4 groupies.
"Whip off", he said to Wild Sal.

Back to back cars filled with females followed Real and Snake Eyes' entourage to the massive mansion where they partied even harder than they did at the club. Almost every room on the first and second floors were filled. Everyone danced to the music that was blasting throughout the mansion. They drank more liquor, smoked weed and had massive orgies. Loud grunts and cries of pleasure echoed throughout the mansion. Bodies were mingled together from the living room all the way to the glass sliding door in the kitchen that led to the pool area in the backyard. They were all over the couches, tables, counters, floors, and inside the pool in the backyard.

The only one that wasn't participating in the spectacular event was Real. He was on the third floor in the master bedroom in a deep sleep with Wild Sal guarding the door.

"Oh shit, this dick feel so good papi", the thick Spanish speaking mami moaned as she stopped licking on another slim woman, who had her legs spread wide in the air with her swollen clitoris exposed.

Dose had her bent over, face down in between the other woman's thighs, with her ass tooted in the air beating it up relentlessly from the back. They were in the middle of the main living room floor on a white Persian rug.

"You like daddy big dick huh?" Dose grunted looking down at her voluptuous ass jiggling as he began giving her his death stroke.

SLAP! He smacked her on the ass.

"Aww fuck. I'm cumming on that dick", she moaned as she buried her face between the other woman's thick thighs and began devouring her honey pot.

"Aww, mami", the slim woman moaned.

She grabbed the back of her head as her eyes rolled back. Dose continued to beat it up from the back. He glanced over at the several males and exotic females sucking and fucking all over the couches and floor. He turned to see two Jamaican women having their filthy way with Snake Eyes.

Snake Eyes was lying on his back with one of the thick Jamaican woman sitting on his face grinding fiercely while the other petite redbone Jamaican woman wildly bounced her voluptuous fanny up and down Snakes Eyes hard rod as she rode him reverse cowgirl. The two women were so beautiful that Snake Eyes didn't think about wearing a condom. He had already gone raw dog in at least six women. Loud grunts escaped his mouth, as he slurped and sucked on her fat soaking wet pussy.

"Hmmm! I'm cumming!" She moaned out loud.

She stuck her finger in her mouth sucking on it as her whole body began to shake. She became more aroused from the loud moans and the sights of the other people in the room having out of control sex.

The petite redbone Jamaican woman was still bouncing up and down on Snake Eyes' 10 inch rod. The sound of her gushy wetness farting and the sound of their bodies smacking against each other echoed throughout the room. Suddenly Snake Eyes throbbing penis slipped out of her wetness and she began having multiple orgasms. Juices began squirting all over his stomach.
"Aaawwww!" She moaned while finger popping herself.

That whole entire night and the day after, everyone except Real and Wild Sal partied and had wild sex all throughout the mansion as if it was their last days to live! They thought they had died and gone to heaven, but quickly came back to reality when it was time to hop back on the tour buses and head back to little ole Trenton, NJ.

Everyone slept like babies damn near the whole ride. They were all drained from their excessive partying and sexual activity. Real, who sat next to Wild Sal, was nodding off when he felt his cell phone vibrating. It was a text message on the screen from Dynasty. *Damn Baby What Time You Think You're Going To Be Back In The City?* Real texted her back letting her know they were just exiting the highway and were now arriving downtown.

A few minutes later, the bus finally came to a stop on the Boulevard in front of the projects.

"Aight my niggas, wake the fuck up. We finally back home", Real shouted getting up from his seat.

Loud yawns and arms stretching was all that was seen and heard as they struggled to get themselves together. Real walked over to where Dose and Snake Eyes were seated and stood over the two. He grinned when he saw their heads resting on one another knocked out cold snoring. He lowered his head near Snake Eyes ear.

"Wake the fuck up! We home!"

Startled, they jerked out of their sleep and looked up at Real like he was crazy. Real laughed his ass off as he ran to the front of the bus to get off.

As soon as Real stepped off the bus, several unmarked cars began speeding up from all angles surrounding both tour buses. They jumped out of their cars with their guns drawn, hiding behind their car doors for protection.

"Freeze!" One of the tall white officers yelled.

The officer was a few feet away from Real waiting for him to make one false move so he could blow his head off of his shoulders. Real definitely didn't see this coming. Surprised, he put his hands up in the air. *Damn, what the fuck is this about?* Real mumbled under his breath as they surrounded him. One of the other officers walked up on Real, slammed him on the ground, handcuffed him, and put him in back of one of the unmarked cars. The officers checked the tour bus and everyone on it, but didn't find anything so they let everyone else go.

CHAPTER 12

Early morning, almost a week later, Dynasty was asleep on the sofa catching up on her rest. Nyla sat on the couch across from her with the cordless phone in her hand waiting for her son to call. She had bags under her eyes from staying up all night the last couple of days. She was stressed out of her mind about the two murder charges Real was hit with. *I need another cigarette,* she thought grabbing an empty box of Newports off the coffee table. "Damn", she said angrily crushing it.

Nyla snatched her pocketbook off the couch and went out the front door. She walked to the store around the corner from her house and purchased another box of cigarettes. On the way home she saw a man across the street wearing a black hoodie snooping around her son's stash house.
"Hey you! What the hell are you doing!"

The man stopped in his tracks but she still couldn't see who it was because he had his back turned. Nyla began walking across the street towards the man.

"I know you hear me!"

The man quickly turned around and Nyla stared at him suspiciously. There was an awkward silence for a few seconds.

"Hey mom!" Snake Eyes greeted with a sneaky grin. "I'm just checking up on everything. You know somebody got to step up until my brother come home. How's he doing?"

Damn I should have waited until night like I started to, he thought to himself. Snake Eyes was at Real's stash house trying to steal the money that he helped him put up.

"He's doing aight. My daughter's supposed to be coming to get some money from you right?" Nyla asked.

"Yeah, when I talked to her she said she was going to come and get it in a few days."

"Ok that sounds good. Listen, please don't let my son know about me using again."

"Your business is your business. Why would I tell someone else about it?"

Nyla felt relieved. She kind of figured that Snake Eyes wasn't the type to say anything, but she just had to make sure.

"Alright now, I need some of my medicine. Please tell me you have some on you right now", she asked desperately.
"I think so. Let me check."

Snake Eyes checked his pants pockets.
"Here it go right here", he said as he pulled a few bags of heroin out of his pocket and handed it to Nyla.
"Thank you", she said smiling.
"No, thank you!" Snake Eyes said chuckling.

He walked to his car that was parked further up the street. Nyla saw Dynasty standing in the doorway looking directly at her so she quickly stuffed the baggy in her purse. *Oh shit, I hope Dynasty didn't see me,* she thought. Nyla nervously walked over to the porch swallowing hard.

"Who was that you were just talking to?" Dynasty asked meeting Nyla as she walked up the porch steps.

Dynasty couldn't get a good look at Snake Eyes because when she opened the door, he was already walking away.

"That was one of Real's friends asking me about his well being", Nyla replied avoiding eye contact, brushing past Dynasty's swollen belly.

Dynasty felt a funny vibe from Nyla but overlooked it.
"Tadasia just called a few minutes ago, she's on her way over", Dynasty told her.

Without wasting any time Real's mother rushed inside the bathroom and closed the door. She grabbed the needle, spoon, and rubber band from the cabinet under the bathroom sink, sat on the toilet and grabbed the lighter out of her purse. Within seconds she made her fix, then wrapped a long sock around her arm. Nyla spotted a large vain in her forearm and pumped the needle filled with heroin into it. She threw her head back and exhaled deeply. Suddenly her eyes rolled behind her head. Nyla fell to the floor and started having convulsions with spit foaming at each side of her mouth. The bag of heroin that Snake Eyes gave her was straight up raw heroin without one speck of cut!

DIAMOND 3 COMING OUT JULY '18!